To Seven

SUPREME BEINGZ II:
WEAPONZ OF THE SPIRIT

Thank You
I hope You
Enjoy!
Gullah Festival
2023
JM

SUPREME BEINGZ II:

Weaponz of the Spirit

BY DAMON THOMPSON

Charleston, SC
www.PalmettoPublishing.com

Supreme Beingz II

First Edition

Hardcover ISBN: 978-1-64990-685-4
Paperback ISBN: 978-1-64990-960-2
eBook ISBN: 978-1-64990-684-7

TABLE OF CONTENTS

Chapter 1:

WHO ARE YOU?

"Mmmm. Mmmm," Lauryn mumbled as she desperately tried to scream for help. Her mouth was taped closed, which kept her from confessing her words into the air. A rope wrapped around her was tight and secure, which disabled her movement. She was tied to a chair. Her hands were tied with a rope.

She mumbled again, "Mmm! Mmm!"

This time, she attempted to pull her arms apart. "Mmm!" She felt an electric shock flow through her fingers and travel up to her arms.

"Calm down," the voice in her head said.

She looked around franticly in an attempt to see who was instructing her to remain calm.

"Lauryn, I'm not there, but I'm with you. My name is Doc. I am here to help you. If you try to get out, you will be shocked by the device that you are tied with. Breathe, relax, and calm down," Doc instructed.

Lauryn took three deep breaths and exhaled. Her anxiety level decreased to baseline, and she focused with her eyes closed.

"Who are you? And how are you able to talk to me? Is Staxx ok? I mean, I saw the guys that came into the office, and they looked like trouble and I didn't know what to do!" she said as her anxiety increased again.

"I have a lot to tell you; you are going to have to remain calm," Doc said.

He got up from his chair and walked to a room. He opened the door and sat in the middle of a rug that he used for praying. Doc looked at the door, and the doorknob locked. He blinked his eyes, and all of the lights turned off. He then waved his hands which, made the curtains close. The room was dark but peaceful. Doc descended into Lauryn's head again. This time, he blocked the anxious thoughts that cluttered her mind.

"What do you see?" Doc asked Lauryn.

"Several men and women. Their eyes are red. Some of them have on white shirts. Some have hoods over their heads. What shall I do?"

"Do you recall how you got where you are?" Doc asked.

"No, I don't recall," she answered. "Wait! I see one of the guys that came into the office! He's coming my way! What shall I do?"

"Remain calm and listen to what he has to say," Doc advised.

The guy walked over to Lauryn, and she closed her eyes and relaxed her body. She felt an instant rush that alleviated all her anxiety. The guy walked in front of Lauryn and looked at her. He placed his fingers on her chin, slowly lifting her head up. Lauryn, with her eyes shut, saw a glowing red light from the inside of her eyelids. Lauryn slowly opened her eyes with fear. She looked into the guy's red eyes.

"We have been searching for you for years. Since you've been born. Now we have you," he said to Lauryn.

Lauryn started to panic as she tried to erase the images from her mind. The guy squatted down next to her ear and whispered to her.

"I killed your so-called Guardian Angel Staxx. I really enjoyed letting off each shot that pierced through his frail flesh and organs."

The man moved Lauryn's hair from her face and slowly licked the side of her cheek. Lauryn closed her eyes tightly as she felt the wet, cold tongue slide up her face. The smell of gruesome saliva lingered on her cheek. Lauryn locked her jaw in an attempt to brace for what was next.

"Lauryn! Focus!" Doc's voice echoed in her head.

"Describe him. What does he smell like? I need details! Don't speak out loud. Communicate through your mind. I will be able to hear every word."

Lauryn exhaled sharply. "One thing that is standing out about him are his eyes. They are red, bloody red. I saw something in his eyes. He stands about six feet tall. He is wearing a truck driver hat. I don't know. This guy gives off a menacing vibe," Lauryn thought.

He slowly pulled the tape stuck across her mouth. Pieces of skin from her lip peeled off along with the tape. Blood slowly dripped from her lip. That caught the guy's attention. He took off his right glove and licked his index finger. He wiped the blood from Lauryn's lip with his finger and sucked his finger. Lauryn spat on the floor to remove the smell of the guy's finger from her mouth.

"What do you want from me?" she stammered.

The guy just smiled at Lauryn.

"My dear…my dear…" he said as he slowly massaged his fingers through her twisted, kinky hair.

He looked back to see if anyone was looking and whispered to her.

"Someone awaits you."

"Who is waiting for me? Wait. Wait! What do you want with me? Who are you?" Lauryn asked as the man walked away.

He slowly turned around and started to walk back to Lauryn.

"He's coming back!" Lauryn thought.

"Get him to talk. Try to figure out where you are," Doc urged Lauryn.

"Who am I? Let's see. The name is Soulek," he said proudly.

"Who do you work for?" Lauryn asked.

"My Queen will deal with you momentarily. While we anticipate my Queen's presence, I will keep you company," Soulek said in a malevolent grin.

Doc disengaged his communication with Lauryn. He opened his eyes and slowly stood up.

"Soulek," he said slowly, trying to recall where he'd heard the name. "It doesn't seem like he is going to bring harm to her. I have to find their location."

Doc sat back down on the floor in a flower pose and engage back with Lauryn.

"Hello. Hey! Are you still there?" Lauryn thought.

"Yes. I'm here," Doc confirmed.

"Did you get his name?" Lauryn asked.

"Yes. Soulek," Doc said with concern.

"What are you doing?" a gorgeous female asked. Her heels clicked as she approached Soulek and Lauryn.

"Nothing, my Queen," Soulek said.

"So...This is the souvenir?" the lady said while walking around Lauryn. She stopped once she'd completed a full circle. She rubbed her hand across Lauryn's head, admiring her hair style. She clutched the twisted hair in the back of her head and pulled Lauryn's hair, forcing her head backward. Lauryn's head leaned back. She examined Lauryn's face and sniffed her. Soulek looked on nervous.

She noticed the tape on the ground and picked it up. She slowly placed the tape over Lauryn's mouth and made eye contact with her. The lady slowly backed up from Lauryn and opened her silk robe to the side and pulled out a golden dagger with diamond stones. She unwrapped a piece of cloth from the handle and sheathed the dagger. She walked over to Lauryn and said, "See no evil."

She tied the black cloth around Lauryn's eyes to blindfold her. Lauryn started to jerk in an attempt to remove the blindfold from her face.

"My Queen, I didn't mean anything of it. I was drawn to her," Soulek said nervously.

"You are to watch her! If anything happens to her on your watch, you will be immured!" the lady said.

Soulek lowered his head in shame as the lady walked off; the sounds of her heels echoed throughout the room, earning attention from the others. Soulek put his glove back on and looked around at everyone who was witnessing the public embarrassment that took place.

"The show is over! Get back to work!" He said furiously.

Soulek walked back to Lauryn and told her, "I found you! Remember that! It was me! Soulek!"

Lauryn was confused that she couldn't see anything or move. She started feeling helpless. Her thoughts started to produce fear that swarmed her body. Her life started flashing in her mind; thoughts of the two men entering the building flashed instantaneously through her brain. She also had a quick flash of Mrs. Davenport walking into the office. Images of her childhood were dim and gray. She started having mental flashes of Staxx and how he'd taught her to meditate and seek God's guidance. "Meditation is when you silence the mind. Meditation is when you silence the mind," Lauryn recalled Staxx telling her. The voice slowly diminished in her mind. Everything became silent, the dark became comforting, and the bondage that held her body to the chair felt convenient.

"Lauryn, it's me, Doc. Your mind is cleared. Continue to keep your meditation active; this will allow us to communicate on a higher level," Doc said.

Lauryn's mind and body were on autopilot. She was fully engaged with Doc and aligned with his conversation.

"I am here," A more tranquil Lauryn acknowledged.

"A lady approached you. Can you describe her appearance.?" Doc asked.

"She was...she was beautiful. The most alluring person I have ever seen. Her skin was golden, and her eyes glowed of a natural honey hue. She wore a long silk robe with red and black designs on it. Her Burgundy hair was braided and gracefully touched her lower back. She wore heels with Egyptian hieroglyphics on each side. When she opened her robe, I noticed her fit figure and bodysuit that complimented her female characteristics. She's a really gorgeous woman. Her aroma is still lingering in the atmosphere. She said I was a souvenir, whatever that means. She wore elegant jewelry; her bracelets stood out to me. They were gold, very detailed, with rubies and diamond stones nested precisely. They were on each wrist. As she entered the room, the men bowed their heads as she approached. She walked with confidence, and each step demanded respect. She is somebody," Lauryn explained.

A cell phone started to vibrate.

"What is that?" Soulek asked Lauryn.

The phone continued to vibrate. Soulek walked to Lauryn and began to pat her down. He reached inside her sweater and felt the phone vibrating. He grabbed it and looked at the screen. He pressed "Decline" on the incoming call and proceed to scroll through her settings. He turned the location off on the phone and set the phone to air-plane mode.

"He took my phone," Lauryn thought. Her engagement with Doc disengaged. Doc sighed as he opened his eyes.

"I found a phone on her. I turned her location off just in case someone tries to reach her," Soulek said.

"You did not think to search her prior to abducting her?"

"My Queen, I instructed Drago to do so. It will never happen again," Soulek assured her.

"Doc. Are you there? Hello! Hello!" Lauryn thought.

Doc connected back with Lauryn.

"Yes. I am here," Doc said.

"When are you going to send someone to help me? I was to travel with Staxx and Myles to South Carolina to surprise Que and Night," Lauryn thought.

"Yes. The twins would have been excited to see you, I'm sure," Doc replied.

Silence entered their minds as Lauryn pondered what Doc said.

"How do you…know Que and Night?" Lauryn asked Doc.

"Lauryn, there is an abundance of questions that I have to bring light to. Your location and safety are what's important at the moment. As of now, it seems like you are in a large room, being held hostage. When you looked into her eyes, what color were they?" Doc asked.

"At first, her eyes were golden, dark yellow. As I continued to look at her, they became red, just like Soulek's," Lauryn answered.

"Interesting. Your details will help me find your location. Do you remember anything about the room before you were blind folded?" Doc inquired.

"It is a large room. Seems to be some sort of warehouse."

It was really dark, but red lights illuminated the large open space.

"I hear footsteps walking toward me," Lauryn thought.

There was the sound of a sharp steel object being removed from its holster.

"Don't move! Drago! Hold her down!" Soulek said.

Soulek cut the bondage from Lauryn's wrists, upper body, and ankles.

"Stand up!" Soulek instructed Lauryn.

Drago grabbed one arm, and Soulek grabbed her other arm and proceeded to guide her.

"Mmmh. Mmmh!" Lauryn mumbled through the tape on her mouth.

She shrugged to try and break free from the men, but they didn't budge. They gripped her arms tighter to secure her.

"Lauryn! Focus on your steps! Count each step and turn that you make. Allow your feet and movement to become your eyes," Doc said.

Lauryn stopped resisting and focused on her body's movement. She began to count each step that she took. She felt her body making a quick left turn. They stopped. A button was pressed. They walk into an elevator. A button was pressed. The door closed. She felt the elevator going down. The elevator stopped. They walked out of the elevator and proceeded down the hallway. Lauryn continued to count her steps. She noticed the red lights getting more intense. They stopped. Buttons were pressed to a pad. She heard a latch lifted up; they entered into a room. Their movement stopped.

"Remove the bondage from her eyes and her sweater," Soulek said.

Lauryn felt the bondage being removed and quickly noticed Drago's red eyes. She made eye contact with him and saw a disturbing image. Bodies lay on top of each other as their souls escaped from their physical form. Souls extended their hands out of a dark abyss; they shrieked in torment as they gradually sunk into the abyss. Lauryn blinked her eyes once. Drago took two steps back from Lauryn, and he stared at her in astonishment. He stammered.

"Who are You?"

Chapter 2:

A SIP FROM THE CHALICE

Doc's concentration with Lauryn was disrupted by a knock at his door. The lights in the room turned on in sync with Doc opening his eyes. He slowly released himself from the meditation stance and stood up. He walked to the door and opened it.

Brix, Night, Que, Fadez, Blaze, Breeze, and Dax stood in the hallway with melancholy expressions.

"Sorry to bother you while you are praying, Granddaddy, but something horrible has happened to Staxx, "Brix said.

"Come in come in and take off your shoes," Doc instructed them.

The guys took their shoes off and headed in the praying room. The room was peaceful, soothing, and relaxing. The window on the left side of the room faced the lawn, where fruit trees swayed in the breeze, groomed precisely. Peach trees, lemon trees, apple trees, orange trees, and a large pear tree all flourished with evidence of God's presence. Birds flew by the window and ate from the bird feeder that hung from a small tree. Doc walked to the window and closed the curtains. He took three deep breaths to brace himself to speak to his grandsons.

The grandsons spoke indistinctly. Doc inhaled deeply and exhaled. His body became relaxed. He turned around and looked at his grandsons, and they all engaged in a "top fifty MC" debate.

"I'm just saying, if Royce and Scarface are not on your list, you might need to holla at Staxx to get an assessment done," joked Breeze.

"I hear you Breeze. Let's not ignore the fact that Cole has been on a lyrical spree," countered Fadez.

"You know I rock with Cole; that's my generation!" said Breeze.

The guys continued to debate as Doc walked over to his bookshelf. He pulled a record off the shelf and placed it on the platter. Night looked on at Doc through his tinted dark shades. It was "Leaders" by Nas and Damian "Jr. Gong" Marley. The music immediately ended the guys' conversation. They all looked at each other, puzzled, and wondered why their grandfather was playing 'Distant Relatives.' What did he know of the album?" As the music played, Doc walked over to his desk to have a seat.

"Are you ok, Granddad?" Que asked.

"Shhh. This is my favorite part," Doc told Que as he sang along, imitating Damian Marley. "Who do I follow? who do I copy? Look into the mirror, and it's you. I said look at me."

Doc sang the entire verse and immediately stopped once he noticed he had grasped the guys' full attention.

"Now that I have your attention, there are some things we need to discuss," Doc said.

"So, y'all are going to act like Granddad didn't just spit Nas's entire sixteen bars?" Breeze asked.

"Have a seat," Doc said.

The guys all sat down. Some sat on the floor, and the others pulled chairs that stood against the wall and unfolded them.

"Before any of you were born, I prayed to God to bless you all with gifts and powers. I'm sure you all have noticed and use them. The powers that you have experienced are just a glimpse of what you can do. You all are going to have to dig deep to search for your true Inner G. The time has come when God will use us for the good of humanity. I watched you all grow up, and I have trusted you with my life since you first started noticing your gifts. You have so much more to offer to the world. The sky is only the view. When I was attacked, God spoke to me that night."

A bloody, beaten, and bruised Doc lay helpless from the attack of his oppressors. His legs were broken, and his ribs were shattered. Doc suddenly closed his eyes and heard a powerful voice that whispered to him, "My son, I am proud of the man you have become. You have a pure heart and soul. You have used your gifts to give in the most uplifting manner. I will bless your next generation with supreme powers! You shall guide them in the path of righteousness. When they need guidance, always be there for them and lead them accordingly. You too will need powers to assist you. Drink this water that I have prepared for you. It will enhance all of your senses and give you supreme powers."

A golden chalice suddenly appeared in his presence. Doc looked in the chalice. He had never seen water so clear and blue. He held the large chalice with both hands. Doc placed his lips on the rim, and in that instant, he felt his body being stimulated with power. His senses enhanced; his brain became fully engaged. Doc felt every living cell in his brain and its potential. His pupils dilated, and his vision became impeccable. He noticed very small details around; he looked across the street and noticed an ant pile where ants were carrying pieces of bread inside of the pile. He gazed three miles down the dirt road and noticed Robert Smalls School. He smelled the hormones that were excreted from an animal that was nearby. He felt every detail in the chalice as his fingerprints stimulated and harmonized with the texture of the cup.

His ability to hear increased as he listened to his heart thump and his blood circulate through his body. Doc looked as his chest and his body glowed from his eyes. His red blood cells transformed into golden cells when the bright light hit them. He heard the high-frequency sound waves of the cells and DNA transforming. Doc's senses where fully engaged and all working as one. He looked in the chalice at the water, which made small ripples. The water settled, and his reflection cleared. His reflection slowly transitioned into a young man and a young lady. All of Doc's grandchildren were revealed to him. Doc saw all of his generations from his grandchildren. He became speechless as he placed his lips back to the rim of the chalice. He took a sip from the chalice and felt God's power. The water traveled through his body and regenerated his bones. His immune system was fortified, and all of his organs were reborn. Doc felt each living cell in his body intensify and maximize his body's potential. He continued to drink from the chalice until his last sip. Doc felt like he was remade in God's image. He focused back on God's words.

"Trust in your ability. Don't let your age determine your ability. The eye will always see you as who you are. Internally know that you are a Supreme Being. Keep this chalice as a reminder that I am always with you. You and your grandchildren will need to become masters of your powers to defeat the soul seekers. You are a Supreme Being."

They all were speechless. The room was silent as they searched for questions to ask their grandfather. Fadez reminisced about when he'd found out his gifts and the feeling of excitement he'd felt when he told his grandfather. That feeling was born again.

"How could that be? You never displayed or used your powers," Fadez said.

Doc chuckled. "Son, every day I open my eyes is a day of gratitude. No, I have not made mountains move or parted seas. There is a time and a place for everything."

He closed his eyes, and the lights in the room turned off.

"That day has come."

All his grandchildren heard his telepathic voice in their heads.

"There are evil forces in the world whose only job is to make sure your lives are ended. They are called soul seekers," Doc continued.

The lights in the room turned back on, and all the grandsons stared, transfixed, at Doc. He stood proudly in front of his grandsons with a feeling of relief. This was the first time that Doc had reveal his powers. The guys continued to look at their grandfather with stillness loitering in the room.

"What just happened?" Breeze asked nervously.

No one answered; the room was silent.

"Soul Seekers?" Que asked as he desperately broke the silence.

"Yes, soul seekers," Doc confirmed.

"Do they have powers too?" Breeze asked.

Doc walk to his closet and retrieved a book from the top shelf. The book was bronze and smothered with dust. Doc walked over to his desk, pulled out a handkerchief from his pants pocket, and slowly wiped away the dust. The book was secure with a lock with an enchanted keyhole. Doc opened a drawer to his desk and pulled out a key. He placed the key in the hole, and the lock clicked open. Doc opened the book as the guys looked on.

"This book holds all of my clues, thoughts, and views leading up to this day," Doc said.

"Hold up, hold up. Does Grandma know you have a diary?" Fadez ask.

The guys chuckled at Fadez, while Blaze slapped the back of his head.

"Focus, yo!" Blaze redirected Fadez.

Doc skimmed through the pages; he slowed down and started moving his index finger side to side while reading the notes that were jotted down.

"Intense red eyes. Able to sacrifice souls from the chosen," Doc read.

"Able to sacrifice souls from the chosen?" Dax repeated.

"Yes. Years and years ago, before any of us were created, evil was born. This plague roamed the earth freely. Breeding hate, lies, jealousy, envy, and greed. In order for them to remain on earth, they made a deal to sell their souls for money, riches, wealth, and all the material things of the world. If they died, their souls would belong to the devil. In order for them to preserve their souls, they would have to seek a Supreme Being that was selected by God and sacrifice the being. My sons, you are the chosen."

"How do we identify them?" Night asked.

"My son, I have been trying for years. My senses can't detect them. It's like they know I'm seeking them; they have a way of countering my thoughts," Doc said.

He continued to turn the pages in the book, and a picture fell out. Fadez immediately caught the picture before it hit the floor. It was a picture of a lady standing in a field of flowers. Elegance bowed in her presence; beauty examined herself for flaws. The flowers that were around this lady gained confidence as they hoped to blossom like her. Fadez eyes had never seen a woman so flawless.

"Who is this?" Fadez asked as he passed the picture to Breeze.

Breeze stared at the beautiful lady. The other guys looked on and witnessed the allure of heavenliness.

"Granddad...who is this?" Brix asked as he looked back to see if Grandma was nearby.

Doc took the picture from Brix and looked at the picture. The guys looked at Doc.

"Dahlia," Doc said slowly.

"Don't be consumed by her beauty, my sons. She is a very dangerous woman. Years ago, before I met Rosey, I met Dahlia. I was a young man trying to find my way around a town that I was not familiar with. She approached me. I guess she noticed the lost look on my face and asked if I was lost. She directed me to my destination and invited me to attend a photoshoot of her. I accepted and met up with her the next day. Once the photoshoot was done, we went to a local cafe and got coffee. We must have stayed there until the place closed. We talked about everything. That night grew old, and we parted ways. I haven't seen her since," Doc concluded. "The next day, I went back to the coffee shop in hopes to see her. I must have stayed in that town for a month. Hoping to see her again."

"What's that?" Night asked while looking at a page in Doc's journal.

"It looks like a poem," Night said.

"Yeah...I had to have been eighteen years old when I wrote this thing," Doc said as he reminisced.

"Can I read it?" Night asked.

"Sure, son, go ahead." Doc confirmed.

"My thirst was quenched briefly. I've longed for the day to connect with your soul through your eyes. Seeking your soul has been a journey that has been dispassionately satisfying and I am willing to continue with diligent energy. I will continue to explore the soul that I've longed for. Sitting in a coffee shop hoping that you will make a graceful appearance and brighten the morning with your stimulating awkwardness. Still, I longed for your soul to exhale the thoughts of intimate conversations that inspire one's soul. Patience and I have become very fond with each other as I longed for your soul. I wait for the day of our soul's binge in congruence of passion. How long will I long for your soul?"

"How can a woman so lovely be so dangerous?" Que asked.

"As you get older, things start to make sense. Time will answer questions and reveal the truth," Doc said.

"The soul seekers are out there and will not stop until they find each one of you. They have evil powers to manipulate and create a path to destruction," Doc said.

Doc and his grandsons stayed in the room and discussed all their encounters over the years. They discussed when they found their powers and the little signs they may have missed along their journey.

"The guys who ran up in Staxx's office took Lauryn! Let's not forget. Staxx and Myles are out there probably looking for her! So, what are we doing?" Night said aggressively.

He walked over to Doc and placed his hand on his shoulder. He felt an abundance of energy flowing through Doc's body. He heard Doc's voice in his head.

"A man without a plan is planning to fail. We have to be strategic and not move off of emotions. I am here to guide you. Be patient, my son, and wait for the signs. God will send you the signs, and when you receive the signs, then you execute," Doc's telepathic voice said in Night's head.

Night confirmed by nodding his head yes. Breeze slowly stood up.

"So, what's the move?" he asked.

"First, we check in with Myles and Staxx," Night said with confidence.

Chapter 3:

PURPLE AURA

Staxx looked around in his office at what was left of it. The destruction and clutter triggered him into feeling overwhelmed. He felt like he had just witnessed a massacre. Everything was out of order as he picked up the pieces to the Eye of Horus statue that was on the floor. Staxx was speechless. He'd never seen it coming, and to top it off, he'd failed at protecting Lauryn.

Myles walked into the office with rage, revenge burning in his eyes.

"Yo, what were you doing in here with Paige?" he asked.

Staxx ignored Myles and continued to clean up the mess.

"She's a client," Staxx answered.

"You know she used to work with me," Myles said.

"Bro, there is a thing called confidentiality," Staxx responded.

"Whatever. You might want to go outside and check on your client, they're outside causing a scene," Myles informed Staxx.

Staxx was in no condition to break up a fight between a husband and wife. He was more concerned about Lauryn and her whereabouts.

"Why don't you go handle it, bro," Staxx replied.

Myles looked at Staxx and felt his low energy. Myles always looked out for his little brother, and he knew this was a time that his little brother needed him. He walked out of Staxx's office and gently shut the door behind him. As he walked toward the front of the main entrance, he noticed Paige standing in front of her husband, trying to hold him back from entering the front door. Thomas pushed Paige to the ground and stormed in the front door.

"I need to talk to that..."

Before Thomas could get another word out, Myles laid him out with a right hook. Thomas's body dropped, and his head bounced off of the floor.

The office door opened and Paige walked in. Her face was bruised, and blood dripped from her nose. She looked at her husband stretched out on the floor as the purple light of energy pulsated from Myles's fist.

"I never did like how he treated you at your place of business," Myles said as he looked down at Thomas.

Paige walked up to Myles and noticed the purple energy glowing from his fist. She looked down the hall as Staxx approached. Myles looked back at Staxx and noticed his fist throbbing with purple energy. Staxx looked down at Thomas on the floor and shook his head.

"You need to seek medical attention," Staxx advised Paige after noticing the bruises on her face."

"No no. I'll be all right," Paige assured Staxx as she dabbed the blood from her nose with a Kleenex.

"Here. Call this number. She's the family lawyer. Tell her I referred you and explained your situation to her. She will help you out," Staxx instructed Paige.

"What about Thomas?" Paige asked.

"He'll be ok. I just gave him a Joe Frazier right hook," Myles replied nonchalantly.

Staxx pulled out his phone and called Lauryn. Her phone rang four times and hung up. He called her again; this time, her phone went directly to voice mail.

"She's not answering her phone. We need to go bro," Staxx said.

"Mrs. Davenport, is there someone you can stay with for your safety?" Staxx asked.

"Yes, I guess I can stay with my girl, Alisa. I heard about y'all's little date, Myles," Paige said, while smirking at Myles.

"Well, tell her I said hi, and when all this is done, I'll be looking forward to taking her out on a real date," Myles said.

"Mrs. Davenport, take care of yourself," Staxx said as he opened the main entrance door to let her out.

"I will. Thank you, Staxx, for listening and helping me."

Mrs. Davenport got into her royal blue coupe with tinted windows and slowly drove off.

"Please don't tell anyone what you saw today, regarding my brother's fist, and this conversation."

Staxx's telepathic thoughts connected to Mrs. Davenport. She instantly mashed her breaks. Myles looked at the car as the loud tire screech alerted him.

"What the—" Myles said.

"It's ok, bro; she's good. Let's get outta here," Staxx said.

"What did you say to her?"

"I just asked her to keep what she saw to herself," Staxx said.

They both got into Myles's car and headed to Myles's home. "Blue Laces 2" by Nipsey Hussle played as the brothers rode in silence. The music gradually turned down in the car. Myles looked at Staxx confused.

"What are you doing? I thought you rock with Nipsey," Staxx said.

"I do…that wasn't me." Myles said.

"Then who was it?" Staxx asked.

"That day has come. There are evil forces in the world whose only job is to make sure your lives are ended. They are called soul seekers."

"Granddad?" Myles questioned?

He drastically pulled the steering wheel to the right to keep from colliding into the back of a car. He quickly shifted back to his left to avoid hitting an eighteen-wheeler, which swiped off his passenger-door mirror. Staxx looked at all the possible outcomes and closed his eyes. A purple aura surrounded Staxx as he engaged. The traffic immediately stopped. Myles's car was the only vehicle moving as he weaved through the vehicles. Myles looked at a black SUV that was to his left. The vehicle was immobile; inside was a family of four. The husband was in a mannequin pose with both of his hands on the steering wheel. He smiled as he looked in the rearview mirror at one of his daughters, who was making a silly face. His wife sat in the passenger seat; it seemed as if she was passing the youngest daughter a snack as she sat in her car seat with her little hand stretching out to receive the snack from her mother. He took the next exit and pulled over.

Staxx blinked his eyes, and the traffic resumed. They both looked at each other, confused as to why they'd heard their grandfather's voice. Myles pulled up to a grocery store. He got out of his car and walked around to exam it. He noticed that his passenger mirror was missing, but this was the least of his worries. Staxx got out shortly after Myles. He rested against the car with his arms folded; as he looked up to the sky, his phone rang. He quickly pulled out his phone and looked at the screen. It was an incoming call.

"Yooo," Staxx answered the phone.

Vigorous breathing echoed on the other end. "I killed you," the voice whispered.

"Who is this?" Staxx asked.

Myles looked at Staxx and instructed him to put the phone on speaker.

"I killed you. You should be dead," the voice whispered again.

"Where is Lauryn? Hello. Hello."

The call ended.

"Yo, who was that?" Myles asked aggressively.

"That was the guy that tried to kill me," Staxx replied, shaking his head in confusion. "He called from Lauryn's phone."

Soulek powered the phone off and placed it in his pocket. Lauryn looked on as Soulek's face expressed hatred. Her mouth remained taped while her eyes were able to roam free. She took a mental picture of her surroundings.

"Why did you call him?" Drago asked sarcastically.

Soulek channeled his hatred toward Drago. He knew he shouldn't have used the phone, but his ego starved for validation of taking a soul.

"What did you say to me?" Soulek asked.

"Why did you call him?" Drago repeated.

Soulek walked over to Drago and pulled out a dagger from a holster that was strapped to the side of his outer thigh. He grabbed Drago by the neck and pointed the tip of the dagger to Drago's eye.

"Don't ever question me again!"

Drago struggled to breathe while Soulek clenched his neck with his large hand. His feet levitated off the ground while his two hands attempted to remove Soulek's python squeeze from his neck. Soulek released his grip, and Drago's body fell to the ground. He started coughing up blood from coming close to death. Soulek stood over Drago's body and spun his dagger around his finger and quickly placed it back in his holster. Lauryn looked on, frightened, as she witnessed Soulek's strength and power. Soulek glanced at Lauryn and slowly smiled at her to confirm his ego.

Myles's phone started to ring. Myles quickly pulled out his phone.

"It's Breeze." he said, looking at Staxx. "What's good, Breeze?"

"Myles, are you and Staxx ok?" Breeze inquired.

"Yeah, we're good. Is Granddaddy ok?" Myles asked.

"We heard his voice in our head! Almost caused me to run off of the road!" Myles said.

"There is a lot to explain. Let me talk to Staxx." Breeze said.

"He's right here," Myles said.

"Breeze, this is Staxx. There is no time to talk. Myles and I are going to look for Lauryn. The guy that shot my office up called my phone. He didn't say much, but he called from Lauryn's phone," Staxx said.

"Do you know where they are?" Breeze asked.

Staxx paused for a moment.

"No. I don't know, but I can't stand around and not look for her," Staxx said.

Night took the phone from Breeze.

"Yo, Staxx, this is Night. Stay put; we are coming to help you." Night ended the call.

Staxx and Myles got back into the car and headed to Myles's house. On their way, Staxx attempt to connect with Lauryn by engaging his telepathy powers. He closed his eyes and blocked out the music that was coming from the car speakers. His surroundings became silent as he focused on making contact with Lauryn. A powerful force rejected him. He tried again. The same force rejected him again. He opened his eyes and realized that someone or something was blocking him from making contact with Lauryn.

"I can't make contact with her," Staxx said in disbelief.

"Don't worry about it, bro. You need to rest. We've been through a lot today. Let's just get to the house and think this over. Wherever she is, we will find her, and we will handle the guys that took her," Myles said.

Staxx leaned back in his seat and attempted to get some rest on the way to Myles's house.

"Soul Seekers," Staxx whispered.

Staxx dosed off into a deep relaxation. It seemed his body was preparing him for events to come. Myles received a notification from his job that read, "Code Red." Myles pulled over to see the details for the code red alert. The alert read, "Lock your classroom doors and stay away from the windows. There is an armed suspect in the school. Take precaution. Do not go into the hallways. I repeat, do not enter the hallways. God bless us all."

Myles sat in his car and waited for another update. Two minutes passed, and nothing was coming through. He looked at Staxx as he slept peacefully.

"Staxx, wake up! Get up, yo!"

Staxx slowly woke up, scratching his beard. He looked around and noticed that they were not at Myles's house. "What's up?" Staxx asked.

Myles showed Staxx the code red message on his phone. Staxx put on his glasses to read the message. He sat up in the seat once he'd read about the armed suspect.

Myles and Staxx both looked at each other, and their eyes conveyed the same answer.

"Say no more," Myles said as he shifted to drive.

"So, what's the plan, bro?" Staxx asked.

"We pull up to the school, find a way inside, and handle him."

"You make it sound so easy; we can't just walk up into the school where there's an armed suspect."

"Do you have access to your classroom?"

"Yeah, I have a key to the back door. We can enter through the back. Once we get inside…we look for him."

Myles pulled up to a gas station about a mile from the school. He turned the volume down to brief his brother on their plan.

"So, we go through the back door of my class and follow my lead."

Myles reached over to his glove compartment, opened it, and pulled out a gun.

"What do you need that for?" Staxx asked.

"Bro, I'm pretty sure dude has some sort of heat that declares war."

"You don't need that, bro."

"A'ight, whatever! Let's go."

Myles and Staxx quickly jogged to the back door of his class. The campus was silent—just the sound of birds chirping and vehicles passing by from a distance. Myles looked through the window of his class and noticed that his lights were on.

"That's strange. I never leave my lights on." Myles also noticed that his front door was opened.

"Someone was in here, look at the door and my desk," Myles said as he and Staxx looked through the window. Myles discretely unlocked the door and slowly entered the room.

"What are you doing?" Staxx asked.

"Biggie said, in shoot outs, stay low and keep firing," Myles replied as he gripped the gun from his lower back.

Myles received another alert on his phone. "Suspect is in B-Hall. Remain in your classrooms and lock all doors. Officers are on the way. God bless us all."

Myles viewed the alert and showed Staxx. Myles directed Staxx to follow him down the hall toward B-Hall. Myles stopped and hunched down; he peeped through a classroom's window. He saw Alisa and her students hiding under their desks. Myles pulled out his phone and sent her a text.: "This is Myles. I am outside of your class. Turn your lights off and place a cover to your window."

"What are you doing out there?" Alisa answered. "Do you want me to unlock the door so you can come in?"

"No! Just do as I said! Turn your lights off and place a cover to the window."

Alisa came to the window and saw Myles and Staxx crouched down by the door. Myles looked up and saw her. He read her lips as she moved her mouth without making a sound: "Be safe!" Myles gave her a thumbs up. Alisa turned off the lights and taped a poster to her window, which concealed her classroom. Myles and Staxx continued to move down the hall. They approached two restrooms and heard a girl whimpering in fear. Myles gestured at Staxx to go in. Staxx slowly entered the bathroom. A young teenage girl was in the corner, lying in the fetal position. The young girl quickly lifted her head once she heard Staxx approaching her.

Staxx slowly approached her with his finger to his mouth, alerting her to be quiet.

"I am Mr. Myles's brother. He is outside. I'm going to take you to Miss Alisa's class. Ok? What's your name?" Staxx asked.

"Skylar," She answered.

"You're going to be ok," Staxx confirmed.

Skylar nodded as Staxx helped her off of the floor. Staxx held her hand as she followed him out of the bathroom. Myles waited outside of the bathroom and demonstrated his composure.

"Text Alisa and let her know that you are bringing a student to her class," Staxx whispered.

Myles took out his phone and started to text Alisa. He was suddenly interrupted by the roaring sound of a heavy machine gun. Countless bullet shells clanked as they hit the floor. The lights in the hall went out, followed by students hollering in fear from their classrooms. Skylar screamed and held on to Staxx for dear life. Myles placed the phone back in his pocket and moved swiftly to Alisa's class. Staxx and Skylar followed him. They heard a chirp from a walkie talkie followed by a voice: "You are approaching two adults and one student. Take them out!"

Staxx looked back down the dark hall and saw a tall slender person with a long, black trench coat. His orange hair glowed from the sun rays that crept through the windows on the side of the hall. He held an assault rifle with both hands. Skylar looked back and stopped.

"Eron?" she asked, confused.

The guy squeezed his trigger that sent bullets soaring in their direction. Myles got in the middle of Staxx and Skylar, grabbed their hands, and teleported.

Eron eased his index finger off of the trigger and pulled out a radio.

"They have Skylar and seem to have disappeared. Over."

"What do you mean they disappeared? Over!"

"I'm standing where they were, and all is left is a trail of dark-blue fog. Over."

"Go in the first classroom you see and kill everyone that's in there! Over."

"Ten-four. Over."

Myles, Staxx, and Skylar stood in the middle of a classroom holding hands. They looked around and noticed the students in the classroom, crouched under their desks, clinching the legs of the desk. The class gasped as they looked at the three standing in the middle of the class. Alisa ran over to Skylar and embraced her with a compassionate hug.

"Are you all right? When I heard the shots in the hall, I feared for your life!" Alisa said.

Skylar nodded her head, still in disbelief, trying to piece the puzzle together as to why Eron had shot at her.

"Miss Alisa, I think Eron is the armed suspect. I don't get it. First Chase dies, and now Eron is a school shooter?"

"My God! What are we going to do?" Alisa asked Myles.

"Shhh. Staxx said as he instructed them to get low. He's outside."

Staxx attempted to use his powers to manipulate Eron into putting down his gun, but there was a stronger force that was blocking him from connecting with Eron.

"I can't reach him," Staxx said to Myles.

A loud thump from a forceful kick to the door demanded everyone's attention. The students all screamed as the kicking and thumping increased.

"Myles, get them out of here now!" Staxx demanded.

"Ok, listen up, everyone. I need you all to stand up and form a circle, holding hands," Myles instructed the class.

The students all stood up and formed a circle, holding hands. The kicking stopped, and a chirp from a walkie talkie went off outside of the class.

"Officers are on the campus! Kill everyone in the class now! Over!"

Myles looked at all the students' faces, which resembled portraits of fear. Shots fired from outside of door. Staxx looked at the door and noticed the dents from the bullets.

"Myles, give me the strap!" Staxx said.

Myles reached in his waistband and pulled out his gun and tossed it to Staxx. Staxx took the gun off safety and gripped it tightly as he stood on the side of the classroom door.

"All right, everyone, hold on tight! We are going for a ride! So much for a first date," Myles said to Alisa, holding her hand.

Whoosh! Myles, Alisa, and the students teleported out of the class, leaving behind a heavy, dark-purple fog. Staxx's vision suddenly became impaired as the fog covered the room. The shots ceased outside of the class, and silence closed in. Staxx placed the gun inside of his pants, with the handle revealed. The door suddenly opened from a final kick. The guy walked in and inserted a magazine to reload his gun. He was confronted by the heavy fog that smothered his face. He squeezed his trigger to kill every living being in the class.

He didn't stop until he heard the click, which informed him that he was out of bullets. The fog cleared, and Eron looked around the room. He noticed the empty desks, bullet holes in the walls, and no dead bodies covered in blood. He dropped his gun and turned around. He was standing face to face with Staxx! He reached for his gun, and Staxx swiftly delivered a blow with his fist, followed by an uppercut with his elbow that connected with Eron's chin! Eron fell to the ground and unconsciously tried to reach for his gun. Staxx kicked the gun out of his reach and pulled Myles's gun out from the front of his pants. He cocked the gun and pointed it down toward the young teenager's face. Eron started laughing, as he knew Staxx would not pull the trigger. Staxx gazed into Eron's eyes. He felt the need to squeeze the trigger.

A bullet ejected from the chamber and stopped in the middle of Eron's eyebrows. Eron looked at the bullet, as it was an inch from touching him. The bullet turned into ashes, and the ashes fell on his face. Staxx felt an aura of invincibility, which gave him validation.

"Freeze! Put down your weapon!" an officer said as several officers stormed into the room.

Staxx lowered the gun while Eron continued to laugh, his face smothered with ashes.

Staxx blinked his eyes, and all movement stopped. He maneuvered the officer's hand off of his shoulder and looked down at Eron. His eyes were wide open. Staxx crouch down and opened the large coat that he was wearing. He noticed that on his shirt was the initial "SS."

"Soul Seekers," Staxx whispered.

He searched Eron's pocket and retrieved his phone. Staxx placed the phone in his pocket and exited the room. He placed his hood over his head and walked down the hall. He passed several officers, members from the swat team and bomb squad. He walked to Myles's class and went out the back door. Staxx blinked his eyes and heard the movement in the school resume.

Myles, Alisa, and the students were all standing outside of the gas station, where he'd parked. Myles saw Staxx walking toward the gas station.

"I have to go," Myles said to Alisa.

"I understand," Alisa said.

"Mr. Myles, what are you? Some kind of superhero?" one of the students asked.

Myles started his car and said, "Something like that...I guess."

He slowly drove off and met Staxx. Staxx got into the car, and they drove off.

Staxx opened Myles's glove compartment and placed the gun back inside.

"I explained everything to her," Myles said to Staxx.

Staxx didn't answer. He pulled out Eron's phone and placed it on the charger to charge. As the phone charged, Staxx typed in the numbers 76857335377. The phone unlocked, and Staxx browsed through the phone as Myles drove to his house.

Chapter 4:

LET US PRAY

The day grew dark as the fellas discussed who all were going to travel to assist Myles and Staxx. Brix looked at Doc as he smiled while the guys packed up to travel.

"Are you going to be ok while we're away?" Brix asked Doc.

Doc looked at Brix and touched his shoulder, and Brix felt Doc's energy as he laid his hand on him.

"Yes, son, I'll be ok. It sure was good seeing you. Wish you all could have stayed longer, but we have more serious things to handle."

Brix looked into Doc eyes and saw that his grandfather was worried; he knew time was the only thing in life he couldn't get back. Brix and Doc hugged as Dax looked on.

"Yo. Who's driving?" Que asked.

"I'll drive," Fadez volunteered.

Everyone looked at Fadez and respectfully declined. Blaze walked to the bedroom that he'd grown up in and sat on the bed. *A lot of memories in this room*, he thought as he looked at the window he used to jump in and out of. Doc walked into the room and saw Blaze sitting on the bed.

"Is everything ok, son?"

"Yes, sir. I was just reminiscing about the good old days, when the only worry in the world was getting back in the room before you and Grandma woke up."

They both laughed.

"I want you and the guys to meet me in the library. We need to discuss some things before you all head out. Go get the others," Doc said.

Blaze left the room and gathered the fellas. They all headed out of the house and walked to the library. Once they got there, Doc was there waiting on them. One by one, they slowly strolled in, and Doc instructed them to sit down.

"I'm going to make this short and to the point. The powers and gifts you are embracing are only a glimpse of what God has blessed you with. You all are going to have to dream bigger than you currently are. You have only scratched the surface of your powers. Trust your Inner G all the time, as it will guide you through your most challenging times. I am proud to be your grandfather and experience your growth as men. What we are up against is pure evil. Keep God first in all that you do. Remember, always trust your Inner G. When you all get to Myles and Staxx, use your time wisely. A war is brewing that will predict your grandchildren's grandchildren's peace."

The fellas all looked at each other to grasp at what Doc was explaining.

"So, what if we fail?" Fadez asked.

"The world as we know it will no longer exist. Your names will not be remembered; no one will write about you in history books. Your names will not exist in a google search. Your legacy will not exist. Most of all, your generations to come will be slaves to the soul seekers. The future of this world is relying on you."

"So why did the soul seekers kidnap Lauryn?" Night asked.

"That is what we have to find out. You all have the skill set and knowledge to locate her and bring her to safety. If it is Dahlia that has her, it is not going to be easy."

"Let us pray. Dear almighty, who has blessed us with supreme powers, we come to you humbly as we prepare to fulfill our purposes.

Please guide each one of us along this dark path. Please let us use our powers responsibly. Let each one of my grandchildren fill their potential as being a Supreme Being. Please allow them to identify the enemies that will enter into their presences. Grant them the courage to step out of their comfort zone and embrace the struggles that they will face. Please allow them to trust one another and depend on one another in their time of skepticism. Bless them all with the tools they will need to find Lauryn and bring her to safety out of the presence of her enemies!"

Doc continued to deliver a powerful prayer, and they all stood in a circle holding hands. The energy in the room could no longer remain subdued. Each grandson began to glow with a purple radiance as the energy beamed off of all of them. They began to levitate off of the ground as Doc continued to pray. Their grips became tighter as their bodies continue to levitate. The purple glow traveled through their bodies, unlocking all of their God-given potential. Blaze's eyes turned into purple lightning as it rapidly moved horizontally. Breeze's looked on at Blaze and noticed the purple glow. He looked around at the others and noticed the purple energy hovering around their physical body. Breeze glanced down to his left and looked at his and Dax's hands locked. He noticed the energy that did not glow on his hand. He turned and looked down to his right hand, where he and Fadez had locked hands. Fadez's hand glowed a bright purple hue that illuminated his entire body. Breeze gently closed his eyes and focused back on his grandfather's prayer. They all slowly lowered down as their feet touch the floor. Doc opened his eyes and released his hand from Brix; the other guys released their hands and opened their eyes. Doc looked at Breeze and noticed his lack of confidence. Night took off his glasses. The fellas all ducked in fear for what was to come out of his eyes. Night slowly opened his eyes.

"I can control my powers," he said to himself.

Night looked around and embraced the beautiful colors that he saw. The brightness and contrast of the book's spines on the shelves stood out to him. He felt an abundance of power in his hands as the purple energy radiated in his palms. The guys slowly stood up and watched Night as he admired the energy. Night placed his dark shades back on and focused on Que as a dark purple flame emerged from his hand. Que closed his hand, and the flame went out. He quickly opened his hand, and the flame appeared. Que opened both of his hands as two flames emerged. Again, he closed his hands, and the flames deceased. Dax walked outside and looked up at the clouds. Everyone followed behind him. Dax gazed at the sky as the clouds turned purple. He then stretched his hands to the sky and gestured his hands apart. The purple clouds then separated as Dax hands moved. The ferocious sound of thunder cracked as the sky opened. The guys shielded their eyes with their arms from the bright light that emerged from the sky opening. Night took off his shades and watched as the bright light did not affect him. He noticed a large rectangular box that descended from the hole in the sky as the sky slowly closed. The guys slowly moved their arms from their eyes. They also saw the box levitating hundreds of feet in the air.

"What is that?" Brix asked.

"I believe it is a gift from God," Doc answered.

"How are we going to get up there to get it?" Que asked.

Brix looked over at a pile of strap metal that Glaze was using for a project. He reached out his hand, and the strap metal began to clang as it maneuvered into steps leading to the small object in the sky. Brix walked over to the first step, and Fadez interrupted him.

"Let me," Fadez demanded.

Brix stepped down from the step, and Fadez took the first step of faith. As he walked up the strap pieces of metal, he prayed to God.

"God, please give me the knowledge and understanding to fully embrace all of my gifts." Fadez continue to walk up the steps in the sky and gazed down. He was hundreds of feet in the sky and felt the freedom the birds felt. Once he reached the final step in the sky, he kneeled down and humbly said, "Thank you."

Fadez then reached out to grab a golden box that levitated in the sky. Fadez looked around and embraced the view. Birds flew around without a worry, chirping and flying freely. The trees stood tall, firm, and confident as guardians of the sky. Fadez heard a whispered.

"Be free."

Fadez slowly stepped off of the strap metal. His body hovered in the sky as he looked around to fully embrace the view. He then began to descend back to earth. Fadez's feet touched the ground as the guys looked at him, amazed. He handed the golden box to Doc that he'd pulled from the sky. The guys all gathered around Doc as he handed the heavy box to Brix and he slowly lifted the top. Doc looked inside the golden box and saw a wooden staff. He gazed at the staff and measured the staff with his eyes. The staff was about five feet and five inches long. He grasped the staff with both of his hands and felt the carved grooves of the wood that intensified his senses. Doc gently took the staff out of the box and held it with one hand, with the base of the staff touching the ground. He noticed very fine details in the staff with his fingers. Doc closed his eyes, and he heard God's whispers.

"Take this staff. It is a gift from me to you. It will assist you in your most challenging times to come."

Doc opened his eyes and looked at his grandsons. They were all waiting for him to say something.

"So, what are you going to do with that?" Breeze asked.

"Wait for the moment. When the time comes, I will use it. I will know," Doc replied.

"I think it's time we go," Night said.

"Yes, it is time," Doc confirmed.

"I'm going to put your box in a safe place," Brix said as he walked off from the group.

Brix held the gold box on his right shoulder and went to Doc's praying room. He walked in and placed the gold box on the floor next to the closet. Brix looked around the room at all the memorabilia. He noticed the chalice on the shelf, as it stood out to him. He removed it from the shelf and examined it. Brix noticed the same engraving on the chalice that was on the golden box.

I wonder what this says, he thought.

Brix looked inside the empty chalice, and he gazed at his reflection as it mirrored back to him. He stared and stared as water appeared in the center of the chalice. Brix grasped the chalice, with both hands securing it.

"What the—" Brix exclaimed as he dropped the chalice.

The chalice hit the floor! The water splashed on Brix's feet. Brix quickly picked up the chalice and noticed a crack at the rim that followed through the stem, collar, base, and foot of the sacred cup.

"Ah man," he whispered.

Brix looked at the water that had spilled from the chalice and bent down; he took a piece of paper towel in an attempt to wipe the water up. As Brix attempt to wipe the water with the paper towel, he noticed the water starting to move. The water deflected every movement away from the paper towel. Brix moved the paper towel to the side and placed his hand in the middle of the spill. The water absorbed into Brix's hand, revealing the screws in his fingers that had been inserted when he was a baby. Brix looked at his hand as Doc walked into the room.

Doc looked at the chalice and noticed the crack.

"What happened?"

Brix was startled by Doc, who stood in the doorway, holding his staff. Brix slowly stood up and started to explain to Doc.

"I'm sorry. I was looking at the cup, and I accidentally dropped it."

Brix handed the chalice to Doc. Doc's senses intensified as he felt the water on Brix's hand and the chalice. Doc reached for the chalice, and Brix slowly handed it to him.

"I'm so sorry, Granddad."

"Shh!" Doc cut him off swiftly.

Doc rubbed the chalice and felt each groove and detail that made the chalice unique. Doc continued to rub the chalice as the crack slowly sealed. Doc handed the chalice back to Brix.

"Look inside, my son. Carefully!"

Brix embraced the chalice and noticed that the crack was gone. He then looked in the inside, and the water started emerging again. Brix secured the chalice with both hands and looked and looked. He noticed his reflection, which rippled as the water moved from side to side.

"Be still, my son," Doc said.

Brix looked up at Doc and quickly looked back into the chalice. As the water settled, Brix's reflection faded out. A young boy's image appeared in the water and slowly faded into the image of another young boy.

"They look like me!" Brix said with excitement. Doc smiled.

A young girl's image faded in after the boys. Brix heart started pounding. "Woah, woah, woah!"

The young girl smiled at Brix as tears fell from his eyes.

"These are your descendants. Your legacy and their freedom are relying on you and the guys to be victorious in the war that we are entering."

"I will not let them down."

"Drink, my son, and fully embrace your powers."

Brix placed his lips to the rim and started to drink the water. As he drank, his muscles strengthened, and his foresight became enhanced.

He saw flashes of a bird resembling a hawk flying in his direction. The image flew overhead, and he saw a hairy shirtless man with nun chucks and a knife dangling at the end. As Brix took the final sip from the chalice, he saw the earth opening up and a man with large black wings crawling out of a hole. Brix then saw a lady removing a holster that secured a dagger from someone's ankle. He then saw the same lady driving two golden daggers into someone's sides! Finally, he saw a mammoth-sized person dragging Doc by the leg while holding Doc's staff.

"Let's ride, Unc!" Fadez interrupted. Brix looked at Doc and attempted to reveal what he saw. Doc shook his head.

"Don't tell me," Doc instructed Brix.

Brix looked at the guys as they all waited for him. He handed the chalice to Doc and informed them all.

"I'm going to stay with Granddad. He will need my protection. Don't try to talk me out of it because my mind is already made up," Brix said, looking Doc in the eyes.

"Are you sure?" Que asked.

"Yes, I am sure. We will be fine. I feel it is my responsibility, as Granddad is up there in age."

"Granddaddy will be straight! Especially with that stick," Breeze said.

All the guys laughed at Breeze, as he was always quick to break the awkwardness.

"Ok, cool. Let's get going," Night said.

The guys all gave Brix a pound and hugged Doc. They walked to a river, where Breeze's submarine was parked.

"Stand back, fellas," Breeze instructed them.

Breeze pressed a button on his watch, and the submarine turned into a flying object that hovered slightly above the water. They all got inside, one by one. Blaze was the last one to get inside.

"Bro, take care while we are away. Call us if you need anything," Blaze said.

"Bet. Thanks, bro. Now go check on Staxx and Myles. Call me when you touch down."

Doc and Brix looked on as the flying object ascended into the air and transitioned into stealth mode, disappearing into the clouds.

"Let's head back. I have to check on someone," Doc said.

Chapter 5:

SUBCONSCIOUS AWAKENS

Lauryn looked around the small room where she'd been placed. The room was dark and cold.

"Hello! Hello! Is anyone here?"

The desolate room answered back with frigid silence.

Lauryn was in a state of confusion; she didn't know what to do. The image that she saw was disturbing. She didn't understand why she was able to see such unwelcoming views. She walked to the door and placed her ear to the door, in an attempt to hear what was going on outside of the room. The cold steel door greeted her ear with an uncomfortable arctic feeling. She swiftly moved her ear from the door. A light in the room came on, followed by a numbing chill in the atmosphere. Lauryn looked around and noticed two large vents emitting frigid air.

"I'm in a freezer?" she exclaimed as she crossed her arms and rubbed them up and down with her hands.

She searched the room for a garment to keep herself warm, but nothing was visible.

"Hey! It is cold! What are you trying to do to me?"

Lauryn returned to the door and began to knock fiercely. Frost appeared on the door from the cold temperature. Lauryn stepped back and looked at her hands; she rubbed them together for warmth. Lauryn's arm started to produce chill bumps, and the temperature dropped in the room. She walked over to a thermostat on the wall, which displayed the room temperature at twenty degrees. Lauryn began to panic as she experienced numbness in certain parts of her body. She looked around again in an attempt to find something to keep her warm.

Thirty minutes later, Lauryn walked over to the other side of the chilling room. She sat down on the floor; she took the pins out of her curls which allowed her kinky hair to fall on her neck to keep it warm. She pulled her knees to her breast and placed her arms inside of her short-sleeved shirt. Lauryn's body started to shiver, and the color of her lips turned dark purple. Her body went into full defense mode to fight off the cold temperature that was gradually taking over her organs. Her heart rate decreased, and Lauryn became unaware of herself; she started to lose consciousness. She started to sing Ari Lennox's "New Apartment" to get her mind off of the cold. Her limbs were numb, and she could not feel her right hand as she placed it to her lips. Her joints started to lock up from the cold. Lauryn was confronted by hypothermia. Her beautiful brown skin was layered with glacial, wintry frost. Her body leaned to the side, and her eyelids slowly closed, allowing pieces of her eyelashes to break off from being frozen stiff. She laid on the dreary floor as she closed her eyes from the bleak room.

"Lauryn. Lauryn." Doc felt the cold silence from Lauryn. He immediately got up to clear his mind.

"I'm too late," he said.

Doc tried to reach Lauryn again. He felt a brief pain in his head, like a brain freeze. A knock at the door disrupted Doc's concentration. "Come in."

Brix entered the room and noticed Doc in the middle of the floor in his meditation position, with his right hand rubbing his forehead.

"What's wrong?" Brix inquired.

"Sphenopalatine ganglioneuralgia," Doc said as he stood up.

"What?"

"A brain freeze," Doc explained. Something cold is blocking my connection with Lauryn. She's not responding to me. I have to find an alternate way to communicate with her so we can find her location."

Brix was confused.

"So, you are able to communicate with her through her mind?" Brix asked.

"I was earlier. She's in danger. I have to find another way. Her conscious mind is not responding. Maybe her subconscious will respond."

"Ok. I'll be out here if you need me for anything," Brix said, exiting the room.

Doc sat back down in the middle of the floor and began to focus. He took several deep breaths as he prepared to connect with Lauryn. Doc felt the frigid cold as soon as he made contact. Doc mentally pushed through the cold to reach Lauryn's subconscious.

"Lauryn, wake up! Lauryn, you must fight!"

Lauryn's subconscious mind woke up!

"Lauryn? Are you able to hear me?"

Lauryn did not respond.

Doc felt her subconscious trying to engage, but her conscious was in a coma from what seemed to be hypothermia. Doc listened for a heartbeat from Lauryn. He heard nothing.

"How are you still alive?" Doc questioned.

Doc listened closely for all of Lauryn's bodily functions, but her entire system was down. Doc communicated with Lauryn's subconscious.

"I will lead you to getting your system back up and functioning. Follow my command," Doc told Lauryn's subconscious.

Doc substituted as Lauryn's conscious and commanded her subconscious. Doc commanded the brain to engage and align with all of its functions. Lauryn's subconscious received the command and recalled how to operate the brain. The brain started functioning and was able to receive and distribute information. Once the brain had engaged, it unlocked its memory storage for Doc. With all of her thoughts and memories unlocked, Doc was granted access to all of Lauryn's thoughts. Doc witnessed all of her memories from when she was in her mother's womb to the present day. Billions of Lauryn's thoughts flashed in Doc's conscious. Doc reviewed Lauryn's entire thought process and what she was feeling up until she was placed in the freezer. Her brain was functioning, and Doc knew he had to get her other organs operating before she went into a full coma.

Doc then ordered the lungs to inhale oxygen and exhale carbon dioxide. Doc directed the liver to engage, and the liver immediately started filtering unfavorable substances. He instructed the bladder to resume its function, and it promptly stretched to store Lauryn's urine. Once Doc instructed the kidneys to function, they started excreting waste. Lauryn's stomach received Doc's command and started creating gastric juices to break down the food into a thin liquid. Doc also directed both the large and small intestines to operate. Finally, Doc commanded the heart to pump blood through the vessels. Immediately, her heart rate increased back to normal. All of her organs responded well to the conscious commands, and Lauryn was back functioning internally. Her outer being was not responding, but internally, her subconscious was responding to Doc.

Her internal organs were functioning well on their own. The frost on her skin started to freeze from her being in the contained freezer for hours. Doc sat in the flower pose, still operating as Lauryn's conscious. This was the most still Doc had ever been. His breaths were precise and moved at a rhythmic pace that complimented Lauryn's heartbeat.

"My Queen, it's been over two hours. I believe it is time we remove her from phase one and start phase two," Soulek said.

"She should be frozen and unconscious. Let's take her out and start removing her organs," advised Soulek.

"I don't want a bit of her blood waisted. Activate the camera to her location. I would like to see for myself," Queen Dahlia commanded.

Soulek walked over to a monitor and typed in a number. A helpless Lauryn rested on the floor, covered in frost. Queen Dahlia watched closely as Lauryn's body lay in the fetal position.

"What was that?"

"What, my Queen?"

"Zoom in! Zoom into her hand."

Soulek typed in a number to zoom the camera in on Lauryn's hand. They both scrutinized the monitor.

Doc felt Lauryn's conscious attempting to command her subconscious. He disengaged from her conscious and allowed Lauryn's to fully take over. Lauryn commanded her fingers to move, and they moved.

"Look closely. Her hands just moved. She's still alive. This is impossible! Lower the temperature to negative degrees. I want her frozen," Queen Dahlia said.

Lauryn attempted to open her eyes, but the ice had sealed them shut. Her consciousness was gaining its full capacity, and she was aware. "Help me," she slowly whispered out.

"I am here with you, Lauryn; your body is suffering from hypothermia. Your organs shut down, but your subconscious fought. Try not to focus on the cold; it is all mental at this point."

Lauryn listened to Doc and removed her thoughts from the cold environment. She managed to stretch her eyelids halfway open and looked up. She saw a small red light flashing in the upper right corner.

"There is a camera. They are watching me."

"Try not to move. Focus on your breathing."

Several minutes has passed, and Lauryn did not move. Queen Dahlia and Soulek looked at the monitor for several minutes and noticed that no movement was coming from Lauryn. It was time for the second phase.

Lauryn looked up at the camera and noticed that the red light was not flashing.

"I think they turned the camera off."

"Are you able to stand up?" Doc asked Lauryn.

Lauryn sat up and pushed herself up off of the ground. The pain that she felt from the cold was unbearable as she fell to the ground.

"February 14, 1998. I know the pain you felt that day."

Lauryn thought back to February 14, 1998.

"Doo Wop by Lauryn Hill" softly played in the background of an apartment.

"Hurry up, lady. You are wasting my time. Do you have the money or not?" a young man said.

"Relax. Don't be in such a rush. Listen to the music and make yourself at home. You know I'm good for it," A young lady responded.

"Yo, I'm out," the young man said.

He got up from the hard sofa and started making his way to the door.

"Wait, wait, wait! Come on man! You know I'm good for it! I can do that little thing you like. Come on, don't do me like that," the young lady said.

The lady began to push herself onto the young man, who seemed like he was about to give in.

"Yo, stop! Who is that peeking around the corner?"

"Don't worry. That's only my daughter."

The young man pushed the lady off of him and gathered his things and proceeded to leave the apartment.

"This ain't right. I can't do this. I'm out! Clean this place up and take care of your daughter."

A young Lauryn stood there, holding a green stuffed frog; her stomach growled from being empty. The young man left the room and closed the door behind him. Lauryn's mom followed behind the man, pleading for him to come back and give her a fix. The young man took the staircase, forcing Lauryn's mother to make a decision to follow him or go back to the apartment. She walked back to the apartment and opened the door. She walked through the mess that was scattered on the floor and made her way to the small room, where Lauryn was sitting on a mattress.

"Didn't I tell you not to come out of the room?" she said, scratching her neck.

"My belly hurts."

"I told you I was going to take you to get something to eat later. You are not starving. You know what? Just for not listening, you are not going to eat!" Lauryn started crying.

"Dry it up! I don't want to hear a peep from you!"

Lauryn sniffed to stop herself from crying. Her mom looked around with rage for something to beat Lauryn with. She grabbed a shoe from the floor and grabbed Lauryn by her arm. She threw the stuffed frog away from her daughter and swung the shoe in an attempt to beat Lauryn on her back. Lauryn twisted her arm, managed to break loose from her mom, and ran to the balcony.

"Bring your butt back here!"

Lauryn slowly backed up on the balcony and tripped over a beer bottle. She slipped and fell between the bars of the balcony.

"Baby!" her mother screamed as she ran to the edge.

Her mom ran to her and kicked the bottle out of her way. She looked down on the ground and stopped. Her eyes stretched wide open as her soul was rapidly satisfied. She crouched down to retrieve the pipe stuffed with little white rocks. Lauryn screamed fearfully as she held on to the balcony for her life. Her mom looked at the pipe with the black burnt tip as Lauryn's scream gradually faded out of her conscious. She looked at Lauryn, and they both made eye contact. When their eyes connected, Lauryn saw something in her mother's eyes that she had never seen before. She saw her mother's soul being escorted by a large angel with black wings. Lauryn's mother placed a golden dagger in the angel's hand, and they entered a dark hole. Her mother's soul was unbothered as she held the angel's hand. Her mother smiled as the force continued to escort her in the hole. Lauryn blinked, and her mother stood there staring at her.

"Mommy! Help me!"

Her mom put the pipe in her pocket. She looked at her daughter as she started to slip away. She spotted a lighter on the balcony chair. She grabbed the lighter and walked back into the apartment. She gently closed the glass sliding door as Lauryn held on with one hand. Lauryn felt pain for the first time in her young life as she held onto the balcony. She heard people screaming and yelling at her, but she could not understand what they were saying. Lauryn closed her eyes and remembered what Mrs. Evans told her to do: "If you are ever in trouble or scared, close your eyes and ask God to help you."

"God, please help me," a young Lauryn said.

Lauryn heard heavy breathing getting closer to her and the metal clanking from the balcony. She heard a voice said, "Hey! No, no. Don't look down!"

She felt her arm being grabbed by a strong hand, which gently placed her back on the balcony. Lauryn felt the pain from Que's hand, but the pain was overshadowed by the pain she felt from her mother.

"See? You have experienced pain. Get up off of the floor and push through!" Doc instructed Lauryn.

Lauryn fought through the cold and managed to pick herself up from the floor. Lauryn felt confidence flowing through her body as she gained strength. She looked at her left arm, where Que had left a burn mark on her at the balcony. She noticed that the cold did not come into contact with the burn mark on her arm. The frost from her body started to melt as she focused on Que's searing grip. She looked at her hands and focused on her fingertips, where the frostbite had consumed her righthand. The frostbite gradually moved from her fingers, and she looked at her fingernails on her righthand. The hypothermia had turned them dark purple. Her left hand felt like waves of fire were flowing through it.

She massaged her hands together and embraced the fire and ice. The light in the room went off.

"Lauryn…Lauryn…Lauryn," Doc whispered.

She did not respond. She blinked her eyes slowly, and her communication with Doc ended. She wiped her face with her left hand to remove the remaining ice.

Doc felt his connection with Lauryn suddenly ending. He felt a powerful force blocking him from contacting her.

"Lauryn! Lauryn!" he screamed.

The latch on the door slowly lifted! Lauryn backed up until her back was against the wall. Her left hand caught fire as her right had turned into a rage of blue verglas. The sounds of the chilling air surrounded the room as the cold mist shot out the vents. The steel door opened halfway, and the cold air escaped, greeting the soul seeker in the face. He opened the door fully and noticed the left side of the room illuminated by a bright torch. The right side of the room was illuminated by a bright wintry mix. The soul seeker looked at Lauryn, whose back was against the wall. He made contact with her and saw the rage of fire and the numbing pain of ice! Lauryn lifted her hands, and the fire and ice mixed. Drago looked up at her hands and witnessed the fire and ice blending together.

"Waaaiit!" Drago yelled. "I am here to help you. If you want to make it out of here alive. I can show you the way. Soulek is on his way to finish you off."

"Why should I trust you?" Lauryn asked.

"You shouldn't, but I don't have to lie to you," Drago said. "I can't explain everything now, but I know what they are trying to do to you is fatal. If you don't come with me, they will be here soon."

Lauryn looked into Drago's eyes; where his soul should have been was empty. She saw the truth and betrayal that he struggled with internally.

"Come on. Let's go!"

Drago gave Lauryn a large frock with a hood. "Here, put this on. You will have to disguise yourself from the others."

Lauryn placed the frock on and followed Drago out of the freezer. She looked around and noticed cameras in every corner.

"How are we going to get out of here with cameras everywhere?"

"Shhh! Follow me!" he instructed.

Lauryn followed Drago down a long, dark hall. They passed several doors that were painted in different colors. Lauryn tried to connect with Doc, but she was not successful. Drago approached a corner and stopped. He peeked around the corner and saw Soulek, along with other soldiers, making their way in his direction. He looked up and saw an opening to the ceiling in the hallway. He jumped up and stuck to the ceiling and removed the access to the vent.

"Here, hold this."

He dropped the cover to the vent to Lauryn and maneuvered himself into the ceiling.

He looked and heard them approaching.

"Quickly! Give me your hand!"

Lauryn jumped, holding the cover to the vent in one hand and stretching her other hand to Drago. He caught her hand and pulled her into the ceiling. Drago placed the vent cover back on and watched as Soulek and his soldiers walked by.

"Wait a minute. Stop," Soulek ordered the soldiers.

He looked up and noticed water dripping from the vent and making a small puddle on the floor.

"Someone clean up this mess!" Soulek instructed as he looked up at the vent.

Lauryn looked at her hand and noticed the water had come from it. Her heart was beating rapidly, and she was anxious. Drago looked at her hands and immediately pulled two gloves from his pocket. Lauryn regained her composure and placed the gloves on her hands. The dripping ceased as she calmed down.

"Let's go," Drago instructed her.

Drago and Lauryn crawled through the dark ceiling until they reached the end of the corner.

"We should be safe here for a while."

Lauryn removed her hood. She looked at Drago and noticed the welts around his neck. She also noticed that his skin had a dry, grayish hue.

"What are you?" Lauryn asked.

Drago looked at Lauryn and felt the need to explain it to her.

"I am what you call a soul seeker. A long time ago, my ancestors sacrificed their souls. In return, they were rewarded with riches and wealth," Drago explained.

"Who did they sacrifice their souls to?" Lauryn asked.

"An evil force, evil energy. In order for soul seekers to remain in a physical form, we have to sacrifice the chosen to the evil force. If the chosen is sacrificed, our days in the universe will resume and be heavily rewarded."

"How is that so?" Lauryn asked, befuddled.

"Staxx, why did you kill him?"

"He was in the way of our mission."

Lauryn gained the courage to ask the question that was heavy on her heart.

"Then why me?"

"Do you not know who you are?" Drago asked.

"I'm Lauryn."

Drago chuckled. "Lauryn is not your name. Your ancestors originate from Kemet. You have royal blood that flows through your body. You people don't even know your true worth and value."

"It's no wonder you are lost and taken advantage of. If you knew who you truly are, you would reign as Supreme Beings. Your God has chosen his people, and yet your people don't even know who their God is."

Lauryn looked at Drago and felt his truth; she felt like she'd been lied to all of her life. She really didn't know who she was; she was a person that was robbed and stripped of her true identity.

"Do you not feel the presence of your God in you?" Drago asked.

Lauryn didn't answer. Instead, she listened closely to the conversation that was taking place below them.

"How did she escape, and where is Drago?" Soulek took out a device and pressed a button. He looked up as Drago's device sounded off.

Chapter 6:

BOOK OF ZAINA

A large jet hovered over a vast field, which parted and broke off below. The two large oval wings folded down as the jet descended. A two-way door and a ramp gradually slid out from the bottom. Fadez walked out of the jet and looked around.

"Aye, Breeze. Are you sure this is the correct place?"

Breeze stepped out after Fadez to confirm. "Yeah, Myles said it would be a large open corn field."

The other guys followed behind Breeze as they waited for Staxx and Myles. Breeze pressed a button on his watch, which engaged the jet's stealth mode. The jet camouflaged with the colors of the field and immediately became invincible.

Night took out his phone and called Myles.

"Yo. We are here."

"Ok, walk to the end of the field, and we will meet you there."

"Ok, let's walk," Night instructed the fellas.

They all started to walk through the large corn field, pushing the withered crops out of their way and creating a path to the end. The field was like a maze, and it was confusing.

"It seems like we are walking in circles," Que said.

"Dax, help us out, man!" Breeze pleaded.

Dax touched a few of the withered crops and they all fell down like a domino effect.

"I see them. Let's go," Dax said.

"Breeze looked at Dax and shook his head."

"Don't say nothing. Let's just go," Fadez said to Breeze as he chuckled.

The guys all followed Dax as they walked past Breeze. Blaze threw his arm around Breeze's neck, and laughed as they walked.

Waiting for them at the end of the field were Myles and Staxx. They all greeted Myles and Staxx by giving them hugs. The guys were extremely happy to see one another, as it had been a long time. Dax looked at the field and walked back to the crops. He dug into the earth with both of his hands. The guys all looked on as the withered crops matured into a healthy harvest. He then looked up to the sky, and rain started showering the crops. Dax stood in the rain for a while and embraced the rain. The guys looked on, amazed, at the rain only touching the crops and Dax. Dax walked off from the field, soaked from the rain. Night handed him his backpack, and they followed Myles and Staxx. They walked about a half of mile to a large cabin. The land surrounding the cabin was beautiful. The fall colors greeted them for autumn's gathering. The sun setting complimented the hue of the cabin and the natural wood.

"Who lives here?" Dax asked.

A female wearing a large indigo frock and silk headwrap opened the door. She stepped out on the front porch.

A group of kids ran through a cornfield, playing freeze tag.

"Ready or not, here I come!" Zaina said.

She walked quietly through the field, listening for the sounds of giggles and footsteps. A young Fadez ran by swiftly, leaving a trail of dust.

"That's no fair. Everyone knows that you are the fastest!" Zaina said.

Zaina began to walk through the field. She stopped in her steps as she felt a heavy throbbing of energy in her path. The throbbing intensified as she got closer, and her hands started to beam.

She glanced down as she almost stumbled over a wounded bird. The bird's wing was lame as it tried to take flight from the ground; the good wing flapped swiftly as the bird's flight instincts.

"Zaina, where are you? You're not playing fair! Come on. You are supposed to try and find us!" Fadez screamed into the large field.

Zaina stooped down and gently picked up the bird and sheltered it in her hands. The bird's fluttering calmed as Zaina massaged the wounded wing. Seven walked up on Zaina and saw her holding the bird. Zaina threw both of her hands up into the air to release the bird. The bird flapped both of its wing's as it flew off into the open sky.

"Tag. You're it!" Zaina said, tagging Seven and running away into the field.

When she was a baby, her mother and Grandma would always say that she was a special child. When her mother gave birth to her, she experienced what she called a miracle.

"Your cervix is at ten centimeters. You are fully dilated. Do you feel the urge to push?" Doctor Stew asked.

In the womb was baby Zaina. She felt comfortable in there and fought to stay in her comfort zone. As she heard the doctor instructing her mother to push, she braced herself to stay inside of her mother. She lay in the fetal position and pushed back as her mother pushed through each contraction.

"Your baby does not want to come out," Doctor Stew joked, trying to take his mind off the pulsating migraine that he was bearing.

Hara gave Doctor Stew a look that showed how she resented his humor, which made him wipe the dry wit off of his face.

"Ahh! Ahhh!" Hara screamed in agony as she felt the urge to push.

"This is not television, where you hear the mother screaming and pushing. Push from your stomach," the Nurse instructed.

Hara looked at her husband, who was by her side.

"Another contraction is coming."

Hara squeezed her husband's hand with all of her might.

Meanwhile in the womb, baby Zaina had maneuvered herself, where she was coming out hand first.

The nurse saw the little hand and informed the doctor.

The doctor immediately explained to Hara that they were recommending an emergency C-section, due to her baby being in a transverse position. Hara did not want surgery, and she pleaded with her doctor to experience a natural birth.

"You are putting yourself at risk if you give birth to your child in a transverse position. There is a high risk of your baby's shoulder dislocating," Doctor Stew explained.

Hara looked at her husband with tears in her eyes. Her husband turned to Doctor Stew.

"Is it possible, Doc?" he asked.

"It is high risk for both your wife and your child. Someone is not going to make it, unless we perform an emergency C-section now."

While they were talking, Hara felt her body losing control as her heart rate decreased. She pushed with all of her natural strength once she felt the final contraction.

Baby Zaina could not fight with the strength of her mother as her hand slid back into the fetal position and her head passed through the vagina.

"Bump...bump. Beeeeeep." The monitor flatlined, and Hara's hand fell down and dangled from the birth bed. Her head slumped over as her body leaned forward.

Doctor Stew and Rudy both were triggered by the high-pitched sound and turned around and noticed Hara leaning forward. Rudy ran to her and caught her before she fell over.

"Baby, wake up! Wake up, Baby!" Rudy said, massaging his wife's face and wiping the sweat from her forehead.

Doctor Stew noticed the baby's crown slightly sticking out of Hara's vagina.

"We have a baby to deliver!"

He immediately proceeded to gently pull the baby by its head until the shoulder rotated and passed through Hara's birth canal. After the second shoulder exited the birth canal, the rest of the body slid out. Baby Zaina was clenching a fist as if she was securing a gift. Hara had died giving birth to her baby. Her heart was not beating as Rudy held her head, shedding disconsolate and blissful tears. With the umbilical cord still attached to the placenta, Doctor Stew laid baby Zaina on Hara. Rudy fixed Hara's arm, allowing her to hold her baby girl.

"You did it, Baby," Rudy whispered to his strong and beautiful wife.

Baby Zaina immediately connected with her mother. Baby Zaina's hands remained in a fist as she touched the person that had taken care of her for nine months. Her tiny fist moved and explored her mother's upper body. Rudy looked on with mixed emotions, tears gushing from his eyes. Zaina's hands continued to move around until they found their destination. Her fists stopped moving once they'd found Hara's heart. Her fists yawned as her tiny hands illuminated. The inside of Hara's body felt the glow from her baby's hand, and the glow traveled through her entire body, making contact with her heart. The glow covered the beatless heart and defibrillated it. Hara gasped as she felt life pumping through her body! She slowly opened her eyes to a little bundle of joy, which was miraculously massaging her body with tiny hands that glowed. Each movement from Zaina's hand gave energy to Hara's body.

"This is a miracle!" Doctor Stew said, looking on.

Rudy hugged and kissed his wife and child as he prayed to God. He too had just witnessed a miracle and watched his baby girl with glowing hands.

"Are you ready to cut the umbilical cord, Dad?"

"Not yet, Doc. Can you give me and my family a moment?"

"Take as much time as you need. I will be right out here."

Doctor Stew bent down to kiss baby Zaina on her forehead. "You are truly a gift and a miracle baby. God bless you," Doctor Stew said.

As Doctor Stew was walking out of the room to give the family some alone time, he rubbed his lips because he felt a tingling sensation. He felt a wave of energy flowing through his body. He looked back at the room, befuddled. The migraine that he was experiencing had suddenly gone away.

Zaina ran off of the porch to greet her cousins. They all embraced her. Zaina was everyone's favorite cousin. She gave a perfect amount of positive energy to combat the negative energy. Everyone spoke highly of Zaina. She was the owner of Zai's Healing Spa, and she was a doula. Her home was elegant and full of positive energy. She had sage burning in the threshold as soon as you entered. The lighting was dim, which allowed the natural sunlight to flourish.

"Y'all come on in," she insisted. "What has it been? Like five years since we all been together?"

"Yeah, it's been a long time," Night confirmed.

As they all settled in, Staxx revisited what had taken place at his office.

"I was conducting a session with a client, and throughout the session, her husband attempted to call and communicate with her. I prompted her to call him and follow up with the session, but she insisted on continuing. As the session progressed my client and I heard Lauryn scream, follow by an array of bullets. I pushed my client down to the ground to prevent her from getting hit. I then placed her in a forcefield; it all happened so fast. We have to find Lauryn!" Staxx said as he walked around the open area.

"Calm down, Staxx. You did all you could have done in a situation like that," Zaina said.

"My Inner G told me to contact Brix. Brix used his telekinetic powers to remove the bullets before they penetrated me. Myles arrived the same time as the client's husband, and they both entered the room. At this time, I released my client from the forcefield, and she was greeted by her perturbed husband, who thought she was up to no good. They went outside for a brief moment and then entered back into my office. He physically assaulted his wife in front of Myles, and I guess he and Myles got into a little scuffle."

"Nah, that wasn't a scrimmage. I knocked him out!" Myles corrected Staxx.

"I called Lauryn's phone, and whoever she's with picked up and hung up. I received a call back from Lauryn's phone; an angry person on the other line breathed heavily! He was upset that I was still alive. He repeated that he'd killed me. A powerful force was blocking me from contacting him or Lauryn. So here where are," Staxx said.

Night got up and walked outside. Que followed behind him.

"What's his problem?" Zaina asked.

"Night and Que feel like they are responsible for what has happened to Lauryn. They have been looking out for her since the day Que rescued her out on a balcony," Staxx said.

"So, you said you tried to communicate with her, but a more powerful force was blocking you?" Zaina inquired.

"Yes, there is something or someone out there, with powers that make my abilities feel insecure," Staxx said.

"I heard Grandpa's voice in my head," Zaina said.

"We all did, Zai," Dax said.

"Granddad has powers too. His senses are enhanced, along with his supreme mental abilities," Blaze added.

"That explains the bullets turning into ashes in the classroom," Staxx said under his breath.

Meanwhile outside, Night and Que stood in front of the open stream in silence. The day transitioned to night, and they began to think about Lauryn.

"Do you think it was a mistake sending her down here?" Night asked Que.

"Naw, bro. It wasn't a mistake; everything happens for a reason. We are where we're supposed to be at this very moment," Que said. "What time is it?"

Night looked at his watch. The time was 5:55 p.m.

"That's a sign!" Night said with relief.

"What's a sign?" Que inquired.

"Five-five-five. That's a message from my angel to ask for guidance and support."

Night looked up at the dark sky.

"My guardian angels, please guide me and help me and my family along this journey."

Night took off his shades and continue to look up at the sky. Que grew restless and headed back into the cabin with the others.

"Is he all right?" asked Myles.

"Yeah, he's good."

"We were talking and decided that we all should get a good night's rest and start our search for Lauryn in the morning," Zaina said.

"We didn't come here to get a good night's rest," Que countered.

"Well, what's the plan?" asked Blaze.

"I don't know, but I will not rest until I find the creeps who shot up Staxx's office and abducted Lauryn," Que said.

Night continued to look up at the sky as the stars started to align. He focused in on the stars as they started to form into numbers. "This can't be!" Night whispered to himself.

"Yo, bro. Let's bounce! They want to stick around and get a good night's rest."

"Wait, wait. Que, go get them and bring back a sheet of paper and pen! Hurry up!" Night instructed.

Que ran back to the cabin and ripped the door opened with force.

"Come outside now! Night found something! And bring some paper and pens!"

They all jumped up and hurried outside. Zaina grabbed a notepad and pencil and followed the fellas. As they all congregated around Night in the dark, he continued to look up at the stars in astonishment.

"What is it, Night?" Breeze inquired.

"Look closely. Do you see it?"

"Yeah, I see stars. A lot of stars," Breeze said.

"Granddad told me before we left to wait for the signs that God will send me. The stars are a sign."

"A sign for what?" Dax asked.

"Night. Tell me what to write down," Zaina said.

"Ok, ok. Here they go again! Are you ready, Zai?"

"Yes, just let me know."

Everyone looked at Night and anticipated what he saw and what he was going to say. They all continued to look up in the sky and at Night. They waited until Night finally spoke.

"37828125. Did you get that?" Night asked Zai.

"Yes. You said 37828125, correct?"

"Yes. They are aligning again!"

Night looked at the stars. "That's a dash! Do you all see the dash?" he said with excitement.

"No. I don't think we can see a dash, Night," Breeze said, squinting his eyes.

"Here go the numbers! 122422844."

"Did you get it, Zai?"

"Yep! I have them."

Night waited for more. After a few seconds, the stars disjoined from their formation and filled the sky individually.

"That's it," Night said.

They all went back inside to put the numbers together. They felt hope and were encouraged that Night had received signs, and they were eager to decode the numbers. Zaina went to a large whiteboard and started writing the numbers down. They all watched as she wrote down the first sequence of numbers that Night had received. She then wrote out the second sequence of numbers.

"There are the numbers. Now let's put our heads together," Zaina said.

"Sixteen numbers total. What do they represent?"

About an hour passed, and they all grew tired. They added the numbers, subtracted, multiplied, and divided. The numbers were not making sense at all.

"37828125. Night! Did you say you saw a dash?" Breeze asked.

"Yeah. I did."

"So, it's 122422844. These numbers are coordinates. They are latitude and longitude coordinates!" Breeze said.

Breeze pulled out his phone and entered the numbers. He typed in the latitude number, first followed by the longitude.

They all looked at Breeze.

"Check that again," Myles ordered Breeze.

Breeze typed the numbers in again on Que's phone and showed the coordinate location to the everyone.

"Lauryn is being held on Alcatraz Island," Staxx said.

"So, what do we do now?" Fadez asked.

"We prepare to go to this location and get Lauryn," Night said with confidence.

"Isn't that place closed down?" Blaze asked.

"There's only one way to find out," Que said.

"Well, I'm coming too," Zaina said as she took off her frock, revealing two small swords attached to her hips. The guys all looked at Zaina.

"Where did you get your swords?" Dax inquired.

"These were given to me by a member of the Ashanti Tribe. On my quest to central Ghana, I landed in a West African rain forest, where I had an encounter with the Ashanti Tribe. The Ashanti people are warriors and vicious fighters. During my unexpected time with the tribe, I learned the culture and fighting style of the Ashanti Tribe. The handles of each of the swords are pieces from a carved tree. The trees are said to have a soul and extreme powers," Zaina explained.

"Can I hold one?" Myles asked.

Zaina removed the sword from its holster and handed it to Myles. Myles grasped the sword by its unique handle. Myles immediately felt the spirit of the Ashanti warrior. He released the sword, and it clanked as it hit the floor.

"Who was that?" Myles asked.

"You felt the spirit of Yaa Ashantewaa. The warrior queen of Ghana. Her spirit lives in each sword."

They all looked at Zaina and the swords.

"Well, make sure you bring those with you on our new quest," Breeze said.

"Back to the island. We can't just land a huge jet on the island. We need to be as discrete as possible," Myles said.

"Who said anything about flying? We will have to travel on water," Breeze confirmed. He went to his backpack and pulled out a tablet.

"Kill the lights," Breeze directed.

He began to type on his keyboard, and a hologram of an Island appeared. Breeze and the others reviewed the 3D map of the island and developed a plan on how they would infiltrate it. Breeze got into his nerd bag and maneuvering the map, zooming in on small details. They also discussed how traveling underwater would prevent possible dangers from guards and security issues. They reviewed the back of the island and confirmed that it would be better to infiltrate where it was less light. They pointed out all the legends on the map, and all agreed that entering through the Agave Trail would be the most discrete.

"Zoom in on the powerhouse," Blaze instructed.

Breeze stretched his thumb and index finger on the map, and the powerhouse enlarged.

I think we start at the powerhouse and quartermaster. They could have cameras showing where Lauryn is being held hostage, Blaze thought.

"Well, it is a large island to cover. There are eight of us, all together. We can form two teams. Zaina, you can lead one team, and, Night, you can lead the other. We will need some sort of device that will allow us to communicate," Zaina said.

Breeze looked down and remembered he had treats for everyone.

"I told y'all I had goodies."

Breeze pulled out a black box with fingernail-sized devices inside. He gave everyone a device and instructed them to stick it on their necks, behind their ear lobes. He then gave them black wristbands to wear.

"Wait. Wait a minute! I have to personalize the bands."

Breeze exited the map on his tablet and pulled up a hologram from the wristbands.

"What should we call ourselves? It's gotta be something that stands out. Something that is unique and, most importantly, something that gives praise to God."

"The disciples," Myles said.

They all disagreed.

"Black powers," Blaze suggested.

"No!" Que answered quickly.

"What's wrong with that?" Blaze asked.

"Dope, but not unique," Que said.

"Staxx, what's on your mind?" Night asked.

"God did create us in his image, so that makes us all a part of God. We all have superpowers and elite gifts that were given to us by God. He lives in us all."

Staxx had everyone's attention. He looked at everyone as they all stood with confidence, eager to live out their life's purpose. Staxx felt connected to them. He closed his eyes and engaged his telepathic powers. "Supreme Beings," he thought.

His thought connected to all of their minds, and they heard him.

Breeze started typing, "S-U-P-R-E-M-E B-E-I-N-G-Z."

"Why did you spell Beings with a Z?" Night asked.

"Because we are God's swords for the spirit. We are all weapons."

"That's Dope! Your head isn't big for nothing. You have a lot going on up there," Fadez joked.

Everyone laughed at Fadez as the name "Supreme Beingz" appeared on their wristbands.

"This wristband is connected to the device; it will allow us to communicate from planets and galaxies far away," Breeze said as he pulled the map back up.

The map slowly spun around as they focused back on the task. A car light shined through the window and quickly turned off. Zaina quickly stood up.

"I wasn't expecting any company."

They all stood up as Breeze closed his tablet. Zaina looked at her phone to see if she had received any calls or messages. There were no missed calls or unread messages. The car drove off as three subtle knocks sounded off on the door. Zaina opened the door. Outside stood a tall, slender man with silver cornrow braids. His face was covered with a thick grey beard; he wore a long peacoat with a black hoodie. He wore gloves with each finger exposed. He also wore black joggers with detailed sneakers.

"Surprise!" the person said.

"My baby brother!" Zaina screamed with excitement as she embraced him tight.

Chapter 7:

BOOK OF SEVEN

A green fifteen-passenger van sped own a dirt road, leaving trails of dust. The van stopped in front of Doc and Rosey's house, and the side door opened. Blaze, Que, Night, Staxx, and Myles all dressed in church attire, jumped out of the van and ran into the house. A young boy followed behind, reading a book, taking his time. The door to the van closed, and Deacon Gee drove off down the road. Church was out, and the guys all hurried home for one thing: basketball! Every Sunday after church, the fellas would all walk to the elementary school that they attended and play pickup basketball games. They called it Broad Rucker. Que and Night were visiting for the summer. Myles, Staxx, Blaze, and Seven were living with Doc and Rosey. The guys changed their church clothes, grabbed a snack, and ran outside.

"Seven, are you coming with us?" Staxx asked.

"Yeah, I'll come, but I probably wouldn't play."

"That's cool," Staxx said.

Seven kept to himself most of the time, reading books and helping the neighborhood kids with homework and studying. He was a nerd, but he didn't shy away from his intellectual capacity. He was an old soul; he enjoyed old school soul music way before his time. Breeze and Seven were two peas in a pod. You rarely saw one without the other. Zaina and Seven were also close. When Zaina went off to school, Seven went through a stage of depression from her absence. Breeze filled the void when Zaina left home. Breeze and Seven were the brightest in the family. Breeze tried to cover his smarts with jokes, and Seven flourished and wore his intelligence on his sleeve. Seven could not attend regular school. The teachers were not able to teach him due to him being far too advanced. While his class was learning adding and subtracting, Seven had already taught himself calculus. He had a college professor that Doc was friends with. The professor came to the house three days a week to homeschool Seven. Even Professor Rand was amazed by Seven's brilliance.

He would often tell Rudy and Hara that Seven was a prodigy. Seven taught himself how to play the piano in three days. He also learned sign language and became a tutor for a child who lacked the power to hear in the community. He was fluent in ten different languages. He always annoyed Breeze by responding to his questions in a different language for each question. This annoyance actually inspired Breeze to learn a few languages himself, which empowered them to hold private conversations in Hebrew and Mandarin.

Myles came around the corner, bouncing a basketball and doing tricks by bouncing the ball off of the brickhouse. The guys all congregated by the dirt road and headed to the court. They wore basketballs shorts, sneakers, and t-shirts.

"Let's stop by Quick's house to see if he is ready," Staxx said.

When they arrived at Quick's house, Myles practiced a few shots in the driveway as the guys waited for him to come outside.

Quick walked out of the house, looking like he'd just woken up from a nap.

"Were you sleeping?" Myles joked.

"Don't worry about that! You just worry about stopping my threes!" Quick countered.

The guys all laughed and headed to the court. The walk was about three miles, but they all enjoyed. When they arrived at the court, several people from the community were already there. Two brothers, E-Money and Big Man were two of the first to arrive. Some hoopers traveled from surrounding communities to play ball on Sunday at Broad Rucker.

"We got next," Myles alerted the others, who were standing around.

Myles was pretty good at basketball. Rumor had it that he could have gone pro. Seven found a good spot to sit as he pulled a book out of his pack. He began to read as the guys played ball. Often, they would refer to him as the referee. Seven played along, even though he was not paying attention. He would often pull his head out of the book to glimpse the game when he noticed them getting aggressive. Fights would often break out on the court, but they remained contained. When Myles and Staxx played together, they would argue…a lot! Myles saw potential in Staxx and would push him to his limits to get the best version of him.

The ball was going out of bounds, and Staxx took off running to save it. He planted his right foot and felt a forceful kick to his calf muscle. Seven looked on as he heard the muscle tear apart.

Quick looked over at Staxx and thrust his hands to the ground. A small cushion of air appeared under Staxx. Staxx fell on the cushion of air and grabbed the ball. He passed it to Quick, who was wide open for a three. Quick looked at Staxx and then looked at the rim. He dropped the ball and ran over to Staxx.

"Aww! Something is not right! I broke something," Staxx said, in pain.

"Walk it off, man," Myles said.

Staxx got back up and attempted to walk it off. He placed his right foot on the ground and felt a hole. His limp was severe, and Seven noticed.

"Don't walk!" Seven said as he ran over to Staxx. All the attention turned to Staxx and his injury.

"Someone get a towel or blanket and lay it on the car hood," Seven ordered.

One of the older guys, who drove, popped his trunk and tossed a blanket.

"Bring Staxx and lay him on the hood, stomach down. Make sure his feet are not touching the hood."

Blaze and Night went over to assist Staxx and laid him horizontal on the car hood.

Seven assisted Staxx with taking off his Reign Man Reeboks and socks.

"I'm going to squeeze your left calf. Just relax."

Seven squeezed Staxx's left calf three times and looked at his foot.

"Planter flexion is positive," Seven said under his breath.

Everyone looked at Seven and wondered what in the world he was doing.

"Aye, yo! I'm going across the street to ask Mrs. Brown if she can call the ambulance!" Myles aid as he panicked watching Staxx's right foot dangling lamely.

Seven gently lifted Staxx's right calf and held it securely. He squeezed his calf three times. He squeezed it again as he looked at Staxx's right foot. Seven gently placed Staxx's leg back down.

"Your planter flexion is negative. Your Achilles' tendon is completely torn," Seven said.

"What? What is the Achilles, and what do you mean!" Staxx panicked.

The Achilles' tendon is an immense and most powerful tendon in your body, Staxx. It's a meaty band of tissue that connects the muscles to your heel. The muscles are the soleus and gastrocnemius. The bone in your heel is called the calcaneus," Seven explained.

Everything Seven was explaining sounded foreign, but somehow Staxx knew he was competent. Seven closed his eyes and placed his two hands on Staxx's injured leg. His hands started to glow with a bright shiny orange hue. The crowd stepped back as they looked on. The healing energy from Seven's hand traveled to Staxx's torn Achilles' tendon. The two pieces of the tendon gradually moved back together and formed into one. Seven continued to rub Staxx's leg as the healing energy moved in sync with his hands. Seven opened his eyes and squeezed Staxx's right calf; his foot moved in sync with every squeeze.

"Planter flexion is now positive on the right calf and heel. Try and walk on it," Seven directed Staxx.

Staxx gently got down from the car hood and placed his left foot on the ground. He felt good. He felt soreness. He stepped off with his left foot to take a step—no pain. He stepped off with his right foot to take a step. He felt...normal. Staxx walked around the court with a slight limp. As he continued to walk, the limp vanished. He then began to jog and attempted to stand on his tippy toes.

"My right leg feels very strong!" he said.

Seven gained his respect in the hood this day. He was no longer considered strange. The guys all witnessed Seven heal Staxx. Seven and Staxx's relationship grew after this particular summer.

Seven hugged his sister and lifted her off of her feet. The guys all walked out and embraced Seven too.

"Four plus three!" Breeze said jokingly as he showed him love.

Everyone was happy to see Seven. He too had been away for years and off of the grid.

"What's going on, cuz?" Staxx asked with excitement.

"I'm good, Staxx. It's good to see you are doing ok. How's the leg?" Seven asked.

"All is well," Staxx confirmed.

As Seven settled into the house, Breeze went back to the tablet and pulled up the map.

"I came as soon as I could, once I heard what happened to Staxx. While I was on the plane, I heard Granddaddy's voice in my head," Seven said.

"We all did," Que confirmed.

"So, is it true about the soul seekers?" Seven asked.

"I am afraid so," Blaze responded

"I wonder why now, after all these years, Granddaddy is just revealing his powers to us," Seven mused.

"Well, we found some major clues about where Lauryn could be held. We all believe that she is being held on this island," Breeze said as he enlarged the hologram map.

Seven walked over to the map and looked on with Breeze.

"This is interesting. This island was closed years ago," Seven said.

"We are planning to go there," Night said.

"Do you think they could be using Lauryn as bait for us? What if it's a trap?" Seven inquired.

"We have to go, Seven. It's the only way to get Lauryn back home safe," Que responded.

"Here, we plan to make two teams. Blaze and Night will lead the teams. Blaze's team will be dropped off at the powerhouse, and Night's team will enter through the Agave Trail. I think Zaina should lead. Are you all right with that, Blaze?" Night asked.

"Sure, why not?" Blaze confirmed.

Zaina, are you ok with that?" Blaze asked.

"Yea, that's cool," Zaina confirmed.

"Ok, Staxx, Fadez, Seven, and Breeze are with me. Blaze, Que, Myles, and Dax are with Zaina," Night said.

"Here, we have communication devices to keep in touch. Blaze believes the powerhouse has monitors where we can locate Lauryn. We will plan to meet up at location X. Here we believe Lauryn is being hostage. We must be discrete and not blow our cover, as her life is in our hands," Breeze explained.

"So, are we going in there unarmed?" Myles asked.

Dax pulled out a bow. Breeze went into his large bag and retrieved a holster with different-colored tips on each arrow.

"Each arrow performs differently; the color code will assist you with each arrow's ability," Breeze explained to Dax.

Dax wrapped the holster around his left arm so it rested securely on his back. Breeze reached back into his bag and pulled out a belt with a small holster attached. He gave the belt to Seven and insisted that he try it on. Seven place the belt around his waist and opened the small holster. Inside the holster were black ninja stars.

"When you touch the stars, they will be charged with your energy. When you throw the stars at a target, they will perform differently. Just like Dax's arrows, the stars are color coded," Breeze explained to Seven.

"I have something dope for you," Breeze said while searching in his bag.

He pulled out a black box shaped like a half moon, and he handed the box to Night. Night slowly opened the box and gently pulled out two sharp knives, the shape of a half moon.

"These are Crescent Moon Knives; they can be used to disarm your opposition with larger weapons in battle. These knives were forged in the mountains of rural China, and they complement the Baguazhang style of martial arts. They too will be charged by your Inner G," Breeze explained.

Night gripped each knife by the black leather handle. He whetted the knifes together and produced a clamorous sound from the keen blades clashing. Sparks generated. Night moved his hands gracefully and with ease, displaying his comfort with the blades.

"You can store them in this custom backpack. That way, you don't cut yourself," Breeze joked.

"Blaze, hold this." Breeze handed Blaze a titanium twelve-inch bow.

"Now gently, gently! Squeeze the grooves in the middle," Breeze instructed Blaze.

Blaze squeezed the grooves in the middle, and the bow extended. From the top of the bow emerged a flesh-piercing blade.

"Now, grip the bow in the middle with two hands and give it a thrust," Breeze directed Blaze.

Blaze did as Breeze instructed; he gripped the bow tighter and gave it a powerful thrust. A blade appeared from the opposite end of the bow.

"Combined with your power, you can do damage from both ends," Breeze said.

Blaze spun the Bo around and maneuvered it around his back. Lightning started to flow vertically from the spear.

"Your Inner G will transfer to the bow once you touch it. The longer you hold the bow, the more Inner G and power will build up in the bow. You can release the lightning from it however you choose to."

Blaze squeezed the bow, and it condensed back to its normal size. Breeze gave Blaze a holster for the bow, and Blaze secured it. Fadez looked at Breeze as Breeze went back into his bag.

"What's in there for me?" Fadez asked.

Breeze pulled out a large sword in the shape of a sickle with a handle.

"This is a Shotel Sword. Forged in the highlands of Ethiopia. Only the most fierce and fastest warriors can handle this unique blade. This blade also has the power to impress the ladies. Not that you need help with that," Breeze said.

Breeze handed the uniquely sickle shape sword to Fadez. Fadez examined the hook of the sword and touched the top of the blade. Instantly, the blade drew blood from Fadez's finger.

"Be careful with that! This blade can cut through steel," Breeze warned Fadez.

Fadez took heed and placed the blade in its custom holster, which was a black leather holster connected to a strap around his back.

"Oh, I just remembered. While I was traveling, I was in search of a brace that will protect your Achilles' tendon. I told the king of your freak injury during a conversation. He gave this to me to give to you as a gift from his country. This brace is made of what is said to be the wealthiest resource on the planet. The brace will protect your Achilles' tendon and give your body the proper minerals that it needs through your blood," Seven explained.

"I have the perfect weapon to compliment it too," Breeze said while digging through his large bag. He pulled out a small dagger and a fairly large dagger. "These daggers are from the western part of Africa. Our ancestors forged the blades in the seventeenth century. They are covered in the wealthiest resource in Africa. The blades never go dull; their keenness is infinite. Your Inner G will be a magnet to the blades and will glow from the Inner G you transfer," Breeze explained.

Staxx inserted the small dagger into the scabbard on his lower leg. The magnetic field from the brace magnetized the dagger and pulled it. Breeze also gave Staxx a magnetized holster, which attracted the large dagger.

"Here I have two axes that were made in the hills of the Congo. These axes are like boomerangs. Here, put these gloves on. These gloves are also made from the wealthiest resource in Africa. The gloves and the axes connect. When you throw the axe, they will return. As long as you have on these gloves," Breeze confirmed.

Myles took the gloves and put them on. He stretched his hand to get comfortable in them. The axes immediately flew through the air towards Myles. Last was Que. Everyone held their weapons and looked on as Breeze went into the bag for him.

"Here is a Simi Blade. Forged by the Kikuyu Tribe of Kenya," Breeze explained.

Breeze handed the lang leaf-shaped dagger to Que. He held the dagger with one hand, and the shiny platinum color of the blade slowly transitioned into a fiery orange hue. The dagger looked like it had just been released from a blacksmith's furnace.

"This dagger will not bend; the iron will continue to heat up as long as you are concealing it," Breeze explained.

"Ok. Is that all?" Zaina sighed.

"I believe so," Breeze confirmed.

Fadez walked off, pulled out his phone, and called Brix. Meanwhile, back on the hill, Brix was relaxing. A startled Brix jumped off of the library couch when his nap was interrupted by a phone call.

"Yo," Brix answered.

"Unc, wake up," Fadez replied.

"I'm up," Brix said, sitting up on the couch, wiping his eyes.

"Y'all made it there safe?"

"Yeah, we are good. Hey, Unc, I'm calling to let you know that we may have found Lauryn," Fadez said.

"Where is she?" Brix asked.

"Night got some signs from the stars and wrote down numbers. The numbers led to a desolate island. It's a lot. Look, Unc, we are headed there in a few. I just wanted to let you know," Fadez rambled.

A silence came over the phone on both ends.

"Unc, are you still there?"

"Yes...Yes...I'm still here. Listen, I saw something. You and the fellas are going to have to be careful. Especially you. You guys really need to protect the golden dagger," Brix said.

"What dagger? I don't have a golden dagger, Unc," Fadez said.

"Something is not right. Listen. Be safe and call me when you get there."

The call ended, and Fadez was left confused. Dax approached Fadez.

"What's wrong?" Dax asked.

Fadez Shook his head and sighed. Dax pulled out the golden dagger from a holster on his ankle.

"Here, hold this. No one must know you have it. Protect it with your life."

Fadez slowly took the dagger from Dax trying to keep the concern from his face.

"Why are you giving me this?" Fadez asked.

"I saw the power that you were anointed with. It is no secret that you are the chosen one. It will be safe with you," Dax said.

Fadez inserted the golden dagger into a holster on his lower leg. They both walked back to the group, and they both remained silent while they packed up. Staxx walked over to Fadez to check on him.

"Something is troubling you, and we all can sense it. What happened on the call?" Staxx asked.

"I don't want to alert the others, but I called Brix to let him know we may have found Lauryn. We were talking, and all of a sudden, he got quiet. He said something was not right and hung the phone up," Fadez explained.

Staxx closed his eyes and tried to connect with Brix. Fadez looked on as Staxx stood in front of him with his eyes closed.

"Brix. Brix! It's me, Staxx."

"Staxx! Go get Lauryn. Don't worry about me. I'll be fine," Brix said in Staxx's mind.

"He's not telling me what's going on. He can take care of himself," Staxx told Fadez.

"It's time to go," Night said while the others stood behind him. Staxx grabbed his backpack and walked.

"He'll be all right," he whispered to Fadez as he walked past him.

Fadez gathered his things and headed out behind the others. Once they all got outside, they stood in the front of the cabin. Breeze made sure everyone had their Supreme Beingz wristbands and communication devices. He activated them, and they were all able to communicate. They formed a circle and closed their eyes. Zaina led them in prayer.

"Most powerful God, who created all the universes and every living being. We come to you seeking your guidance as we prepare for battle. Oh, God, please anoint us with courage and knowledge as we embark on our journey."

As Zaina continued to pray, they started to glow in a purple hue and levitate. Breeze opened his eyes and heard Zaina praying indistinctly. He looked at his body, and he too had the glow! Breeze felt God's power showering on him as his body became anointed.

"I have the glow!" Breeze whispered to himself.

They all opened their eyes and walked to the large field, where the jet was hidden. Breeze pressed a code on his watch, and the large jet became visible. They all entered the jet from the bottom ramp. Breeze sat in the pilot seat, and Seven sat beside him as his copilot. He flicked on several switches, which engaged the lights on the jet. He pressed several buttons that started the jet. The jet slowly ascended above the field as the wings opened. Breeze looked at Seven, and Seven nodded. The jet quickly took off before camouflaging with the dark sky.

The lights in the library went off. Brix slowly stood up and walked to the door; outside, everything was pitch black. All the streetlights were out. Brix looked over at his grandparents' house and saw that a light was on. As he headed there, the light in the house went out! Brix looked around as he heard footsteps. He saw pairs of red eyes surrounding him, and he heard guns being cocked and swords being drawn.

Chapter 8:

THE GOLDEN DAGGER

Drago fumbled through his pants pocket and pulled out his phone to silence it. Lauryn quickly removed her glove and snatched the phone out of Drago's hand. The glacial cold from her hand froze the phone all the way through and it immediately stopped. Soulek continued to look up at the ceiling; he gestured his soldiers to move up in two directions.

"What do we do now?" Lauryn whispered.

"Follow me!" Drago instructed Lauryn.

Drago picked up the pace as he crawled to another vent. He looked down through the vent and noticed that he was at an exit. He removed the vent and slowly lowered himself out of the ceiling. Drago examined the room and signaled Lauryn that it was safe to come out.

"Can you give me a hand?" Lauryn asked.

Drago looked up to Lauryn and helped her down out of the ceiling. When her feet touched the ground, their eyes connected. Drago gazed into Lauryn's eyes and saw her true identity.

"Please remember my change of heart and acts of service," Drago pleaded.

Lauryn remained silent. She blinked her eyes and regained her focus.

"How am I able to see such images?" she asked Drago.

Drago didn't answer as he slowly pulled two daggers from his side. He slowly opened the door, instructing Lauryn to follow behind him. In the dark hall were three soul seekers armed with guns. Drago took off running in their direction, and he threw one of the daggers swiftly, and it pierced through the first soul seeker's neck. The second soul seeker pulled out a communication device and attempted to alert the others. While crouching down, Drago threw the other dagger, which went through the walkie talkie and the soul seeker's hand. He immediately pulled the dagger out of the neck of the first soul seeker, and he tossed it at the neck of the third soul seeker, who began shooting at them. The third soul seeker dropped! Drago hurried over to the second soul seeker and removed the dagger from his hand.

"Traitor!" the soul seeker yelled out before Drago inserted the blade through his internal jugular vein.

Lauryn stood back and watched as Drago picked up the gun. Lauryn had a mental flash of the gun. She thought back to Drago entering the office with it.

"Come on, let's go," Drago instructed Lauryn.

Lauryn looked at the gun and thought of Staxx. She slowly took a few steps back as her skepticism for Drago increased.

"We have to go now! More are on the way!" Drago urged.

Lauryn looked back and saw more soul seekers coming.

"Let's go!" Drago demanded.

He grabbed Lauryn's hand and ran down the hall. Lauryn quickly glimpsed the cells they passed by.

"We have to make it outside! Follow me! Hurry!" he said.

"A death blow to the internal jugular vein. So, he chose his side. I'm impressed. I didn't know he had it in him." Soulek chuckled as he crouched down to examine the body. "Lock down the island! Find the souvenir and Drago, and bring them both to me…alive!" Soulek said through his communication device.

Heavy metal armor lowered on all the doors and windows, preventing anyone to enter or exit. Drago and Lauryn ran to the exit door, watching the metal armor lowering over the door.

"They locked down the island!" Drago said punching the metal door.

"Where are we?" Lauryn asked.

Drago looked at Lauryn as all the lights on the hall turned red. He gripped his weapon and responded, "Ile Du Diable."

The footsteps got closer, and the pair of red eyes intensified. Brix looked around, as he felt cornered.

"I'm not going out like this," he whispered to himself.

The streetlights came back on, and he saw what he was up against. Several men dressed in black attire surrounded him; they all were strapped with guns. Brix calmly looked around and saw more scrap metal that Glaze had on the lawn. He immediately crouched down and covered his head. The pieces of scrap metal flew in Brix's direction, knocking the soul seekers down! The scrap metal formed a shelter around Brix that resembled a metal igloo. Shots were fired at the shelter; the layers of metal prevented the shots from entering.

"Think, think, think!" Brix said to himself as he looked around the small shelter.

He saw a small metal plaque from Aunt Ronnie inscribed with Psalms 28:7: "The Lord is my strength and my shield; my heart trusted in him, and I am helped: therefore my heart greatly rejoiceth; and with my song will I praise him."

Brix flinched as the bullets continued to bounce off of the shelter.

"The Lord is my shield," he said slowly.

Brix pulled a piece of metal from the shelter wall; he began to bend and mold it until it shaped a Zulu shield. He took off his belt and attached it to the inside of the shield for grip. The bullets continued to pierce the shelter, faster and with more force. Brix heard the chattering cease, and a voice said, "Step aside!"

Brix held the shield with both hands and braced himself for what was to come.

The shelter shattered from the forceful impact.

Brix lain on the ground with the shield on his right arm. His hearing was affected from the blast, as he only heard a muffled ringing sound. He looked around at the smoke from the blast, which floated freely around him. Brix regained his composure, he slowly stood on one knee. A colossal man walked through the crowd, wearing a white ski mask, clutching a grenade launcher. He pulled a large grenade from his belt and folded the barrel of the launcher down to reload. He inserted the grenade into the barrel as Brix looked up. As the guy locked the barrel back in place, he gripped the M79 with one hand. Brix quickly hit the M79 with the shield, causing it to fly out of the guy's hand. Brix then began to engage in battle with the soul seekers. He blocked their attacks with his shield and countered with force. Shots flew at Brix from every direction, and he used his shield for protection and to engage in close combat. Once Brix engaged in close combat, he didn't give the soul seekers a chance to draw or use their weapons. He walked over to one of the soul seekers, who was slowly getting off of the ground, and Brix waved the shield with all of his might, connecting with the soul seeker's face. The bones in his face shattered, and his eye flew out of its socket.

Brix looked around, breathing heavily, full of rage.

"What's good? Is that all you got?"

The soul seekers crawled and moaned as Brix confessed his victory. Brix walked over to another soul seeker, who was crawling on all four like a beast. He aggressively stood up and received an uppercut to his chin. The cracking sound of the occipital bone shattering alerted the other soul seekers as they began to flee. Brix looked down to the soul seeker, who miraculously was standing up with a cracked skull.

"What the—" he exclaimed.

Brix remembered his grandparents, and he ran to the house. The back door was locked, so he gave it a forceful kick, knocking the door off of the hinges.

"Granddaddy! Grandmama!" he yelled as he searched through the house. "I'm too late!"

Brix opened the door to Doc's praying room, and he looked around, as he noticed the room was torn apart. The shelves were knockdown, and every item in the closet was on the floor. He looked for the chalice and Doc's staff, but they were nowhere to be found. Brix was startled by movement coming from the front room, so he dropped his shield and ran to the front. He ran into an ambush! The White Skully soul seeker stood in the middle of the front room while the others attacked Brix. Brix fought them, tossing them through windows and out of the door. Brix looked around as he had made it outside; he was outnumbered.

"Surrender!" the White Skully said to Brix.

Brix was exhausted; he breathed heavily. The White Skully pulled out a handgun from his side and loaded it with two needles filled with gray liquid. He pointed the gun at Brix as a red dot appeared on his chest. Brix looked down at the red dot. With the last bit of energy he had, he summoned some strength and ran toward the White Skully.

The White Skully squeezed the trigger twice, and two needles landed where the red dot was planted.

"Let's see his responds to the Zun Serum."

Brix stopped as the needles stunned him; he pulled the needles out as he approached with heavy steps. The White Skully backed up and loaded more ammo, and he shot Brix with three more needles, one in his neck, one in his face, and one in his chest. Brix dropped to his knees and slowly pulled the needles out of his face and neck. The gray liquid that was in the needle was flowing into his blood stream. He felt weakened as he looked down and pulled the last needle out. Gray residue smeared his shirt where the needle had been injected. He felt powerless and weak; all of his strength was drained.

"What did you do to me?" Brix asked as he looked up with a blurry vision.

The White Skully grabbed Brix by the collar of his shirt.

"The Zun Serum will drain your powers. Where is Doc?"

At this moment, Brix knew that his grandparents were safe. He smiled and laughed, even though he felt the excruciating agony from his rib cage.

"You got me messed up," Brix squeezed out as he coughed up blood and green discharge.

This was the answer that the White Skully did not want; he pulled out a pistol from his back and slapped it across Brix's face.

"Mmmm," Brix mumbled in pain.

"Now that I have your attention, where is Doc and the wooden staff?" The White Skully asked as he casually pulled back the hammer.

Brix's left eye was closed from the blows he'd received. He looked at the White Skully; he was surrounded by evil. With his good eye, he looked over the White Skully's shoulder and saw something approaching from a distance in the sky. The White Skully's voice faded out as Brix focused on a large bird.

"Eeeeeeeeee!" the large bird shrieked as it flew closer. Its screech became ear splitting.

The White Skully quickly turned around, distracted by the noise. The bird sunk its eight serrated talons into the neck of the White Skully and lifted him off of the ground. The bird flew in a circle with the White Skully's body dangling from its talons. The bird released the White Skully's neck, and the soul seekers cleared the way. The White Skully's body descended from the sky and landed awkwardly in front of Brix. The large bird circled back around and began to pick off the other soul seekers, who ran for cover. Brix's Inner G was low; he reached out his hand in an attempt to attract a piece of metal. The metal didn't move, and his eyelids slowly lowered, and his hand rested on the ground.

"Eeeeeeee!"

The large bird came in for a landing. A fragile Brix opened his eyes. The bird stood five feet tall! Beautiful dark brown feathers were neatly laid on top of the bird's back. All of the feathers were earth colors.

"Kreeear!" the bird screamed as it broad wings stretched out, displaying its pale belly.

Brix had summoned enough Inner G to focus on the bird, and he noticed the bird's yellow legs. A holster had been tied to its ankle. At the top of the holster shined the golden handle to a dagger. The yellowish, rust-colored eyes gazed at Brix.

"I know those eyes," Brix whispered to himself.

He noticed the short, wide tail of the bird and its dark reddish hue.

"A red-tailed hawk," Brix uttered.

"How are we going to get out of here?" a frantic Lauryn asked.

Drago looked up at the ceiling to see if there was another vent. He looked at Lauryn's hand and the ceiling again.

"You are going to burn a hole in the ceiling!"

"What?"

"Yes! Burn a hole in the ceiling. You can't burn through those doors. That is our only way out of here. Make a passage through the ceiling, and we will crawl our way to the other side. On the other side of this door is our exit."

Lauryn slipped her left hand out of the glove. Without warning, she reached for the sky, and a furious fire gushed from her hand! The fire rapidly spread over the entire ceiling.

"Put it out quickly! Hurry!" Drago instructed her.

Lauryn removed her other glove and stretched her hand out to where the fire was spreading. The ice from her hand captured the fire. Lauryn and Drago looked up at the ceiling in astonishment. The fire was still flaming, even with the ice.

"How is this possible? The fire is trapped in the ice!" Drago said.

Lauryn did not have the words to explain what she had done or was able to do.

"I don't know. I don't know what is going on with me. It seems like, ever since I heard Doc in my head and he spoke to me, things have been weird," Lauryn said.

Drago looked at Lauryn.

"You are able to communicate with your mind. And you did say Doc, right?" Drago followed up.

"Yee…es." Lauryn hesitated; she realized that she had revealed too much.

Drago quickly changed the subject. He quickly jumped up to the open pathway in the ceiling that Lauryn created. Drago pulled out a dagger and started to chip at the ice that was blocking the pathway. The sheltered fire in the ice fell onto the ground and exploded as Drago chipped it away. He looked down as the small explosion alerted him. Lauryn stepped to the side as the fiery ice dropped, and she threw on her hood and jumped up to grab Drago's hand. Drago pulled Lauryn up into the ceiling, and they proceeded to crawl to the other side of the door.

"There is a basement in this room that leads outside. The basement door is covered by a large statue. If we can make it to the basement, we can escape."

A large fist punched through the ceiling. Two large hands gripped Lauryn and Drago by the legs. The ceiling collapsed. Lauryn screamed as her body was yanked from the ceiling and collided with the floor! Drago was quickly apprehended by his fellow soul seekers and placed in an electrical restraint.

"Ahhh!" Drago screamed as the electricity ate through his flesh!

Lauryn moved drastically in an attempt to loosen the vice grip from her ankle. The dust from the debris cleared, and Lauryn noticed that her ankle was being held by Soulek.

"We have the souvenir. I repeat, we have the souvenir."

The metal armor on the door was suddenly lifted, and the door opened. Queen Dahlia walked in the room, demanding attention from everyone. Lauryn watched as Queen Dahlia made her presence felt in the room, as she gracefully opened her long coat to retrieve a golden dagger.

"Thank you," she said to Soulek in a sarcastic tone.

"What do you want with me?" Lauryn inquired.

Queen Dahlia ignored Lauryn and walked in Drago's direction, and Drago flinched in an attempt to break the restraints.

"Drago, son of Draigen. Your father would be so disappointed in you. Why the sudden change of heart?" Dahlia asked while resting the tip of the dagger against Drago's neck.

"What's in the dark must come to light. I can no longer be led into a path of destruction. My destiny is inevitable, but my loyalty to you ends this day. I will no longer adhere to your menacing ways. This generational curse ends today!"

Drago swallowed. He looked over at Lauryn.

"I'm sorry," he mouthed.

Queen Dahlia held Drago by the head and turned to face Lauryn. She dragged her dagger across Drago's neck.

Lauryn showed no emotions as Drago's head slid off his body. Queen Dahlia released her grip from Drago's head and wiped the blood off her dagger with a cloth. The golden dagger glimmered, polished with Drago's blood. Lauryn noticed the statue that was covering the basement. She glanced at Soulek's arm, which continued to restrain her leg. She quickly removed her gloves and touched Soulek's massive hand. Soulek's hand and entire arm ignited in flames. Soulek released Lauryn and waved his arm rapidly to put out the fire.

"Get her!" Queen Dahlia screamed.

Lauryn maneuvered her way to the statue by icing the floor and sliding on her back. She threw flames at the soul seekers to fight them off. She made it behind the statue and noticed the door to the tunnel. With both hands, she formed fire and ice and sent a mixture of both elements toward the soul seekers and Queen Dahlia. Dahlia took shelter, avoiding the fire icepicks. The fire danced on the flesh of the soul seekers, and the ice captured them, instantly freezing them in their tracks. Lauryn opened the door and exited the room. The soul seekers' flesh blistered and burned inside of the glasslike, glacial ice. Queen Dahlia walked to one of the soul seekers, and she and an anguished Soulek looked on as the soldiers burned inside of the ice.

"Shall we call him, my Queen?" Soulek asked.

"Don't be so easily defeated! Send word to Lord Salvo, the Fallen Angel. He owes me a favor."

Queen Dahlia walked to the tunnel. She removed her long coat and entered. Soulek followed behind her and closed the door.

Deep in the Dark Realm, clanging metal echoed through the hall. A large dark shadow emerged, displaying his massive black wings. Bright sparks bounced off the anvil from the hammer as it forged metal spikes. He picked up a glove and welded the spikes onto it. He slipped the scorching hot glove on his hand and was unbothered by the lava, that oozed onto his flesh. He looked at his palm and three metal claws slid out of the glove.

The large hawk began to flap its wings. Feathers shed as the hawk continued to flap and scream. The hawk covered its body with its large wings, and suddenly, the wings started to change into brown arms! The arms slowly moved from covering the head, and the entire hawk's body slowly transformed into a lady! Brix looked on, stunned.

"Egypt?" he asked, confused.

Chapter 9:

BOOK OF EGYPT

The earth's eyes were slowly opening as the sun rose. The fresh smell of infant flowers blossoming attracted the elders who looked forward to entering their gardens. The animals were awakened from the warmer temperatures. The butterflies were resettling, the leaves were aspiring, and the air was recognized by longer days. God's little messenger landed on a windowsill and led a peaceful piece that alerted all…new beginnings were upon us.

The schools were out for spring break, and the kids loved this time of year to sleep in. A pleasant aroma of butter, honey, and milk wafted through the house and floated through Egypt's nostrils. She was suddenly awakened.

"Are you making homemade biscuits?" she yelled from the room down the hall.

Her inquiry was drowned out by the sounds of Bob Marley's "Three Little Birds." Egypt got out of bed and headed to the kitchen; the house was spotless! The wooden floors shined from a Pine-Sol finish. Egypt loved the smell of a clean house and fresh homemade biscuits; it was complimentary to a Saturday morning.

"Good morning, Aunt Beck," a jovial Egypt greeted.

"Why couldn't you get out of that bed this morning? I call yo name fo times. And I know you heard me," Aunt Beck responded.

"I'm sorry. I was really tired."

"Go wash yo mouth and face and come eat."

"Yes, ma'am."

Aunt Beck watched over Egypt while her mother worked. Egypt stayed with Aunt Beck during school breaks and just about every weekend. Aunt Beck was actually Egypt's grand aunt. She took a liking to Egypt and her willingness to learn. Every weekend, Aunt Beck and Egypt would go shopping for the community. Aunt Beck owned a corner store where you could get just about anything. Egypt worked in the store with Aunt Beck every day after school and on the weekends. Aunt Beck taught her the value of money and how to run a business. Even though she credited several people in the community, she loved the fact that she was helping someone in need.

"Egypt, take these plates for Rosey and Doc while dey hot."

"Yes, ma'am."

Egypt picked up the two plates and headed out the back door. Several birds where on the porch, eating from a bird feeder that Uncle Two Thumb made. Uncle Two Thumb was a master carpenter and fisherman. He could build anything from scratch; he just needed his space and time to think and, of course, good music. Egypt placed the food to the side and removed some of the bird food from the feeder. The birds hopped into her hands and ate from her palm. A red robin alighted on Egypt's shoulder and started chirping. Egypt laughed as the robin chirped.

"Egypt! Take that food and leave dem birds lone!" Aunt Beck yelled from the hallway, both hands on her waist.

"I wonda bout that gal sometime. She acts cracky, but I love 'em so," Aunt Beck said while chuckling.

Egypt was startled, and the red robin flew away.

"See you later!" she yelled as the robin disappeared into a tree.

She gathered the plates and jumped off of the porch. Doc and Rosey's house was next door to Aunt Beck's. Dax and Breeze were cutting the grass and trimming the hedges. Doc had them up early working in the yard. Uncle Glaze was blasting music from his trailer. The Gap Band's "Early in the morning" played while the guys cleaned. He sat on the steps, watching the guys; this was his way of getting back at them, passive-aggressively.

"Hey, ya'll," Egypt greeted the fellas.

"What's up, Egypt? Did you pass that science test?" Dax asked.

"Yeah! I got an A+ on it."

"Can you give me the answers? I have to take it over when we go back to school."

"That will be ten dollars. If you stop daydreaming about Shay, maybe you can focus on your lesson." They both laughed.

"Are you going to give me the answers or not?"

"I guess!"

"Say, man. You want to hurry up here so we can get the day started?" Breeze chimed in.

Egypt walked into the house through the back door. Brix and Doc were in the kitchen, talking. Grandma was on the phone with Aunt Beck.

"Good morning, Granddaddy! Good morning, Brix."

"Hey, baby," Doc said.

"What's up, little cuz," Brix said.

"Aunt Beck made you and Grandma some breakfast."

"Oh, thank you, baby. Put it on the table. Rosey in the back."

Egypt walked down the hall to Rosey and Doc's room. She knocked on the door softly.

"Come in."

"I'll call you back, Beck, yeah, yeah. I sholl will. He right in here. Ok, bye."

"Good morning, Grandma. I put your breakfast on the table."

"You look pretty this morning. You taking care yourself, baby?"

"Yes ma'am."

"Go in that closet and get that bag out the corner for me." Egypt went to the closet and saw a light brown grocery bag. She handed the bag to Rosey, and she pulled out two large bags of bird food.

"I know you like to feed those red robins. feed 'em as much as you want."

Rosey laughed.

"I used to love to listen to the birds sing in the morning when I was your age. Every spring, me and my stubborn boy use to plant a garden and listen to the birds sing while we feed 'em. I sholl miss dem days."

Rosey went to the window, where she had a bird feeder, and she topped off the food and waited for about fifteen seconds to see if the red robins would come. No birds graced the window with their presence. Egypt looked at her grandma and felt her emptiness. She wanted to help her grandma feel the joy she'd once felt from the birds.

"It's ok, Grandma," Egypt said as she walked by her grandma and hugged her.

Egypt prayed to God to allow the birds to brighten her grandma's morning and fill her soul with the peaceful melodies. Her prayer was short and sincere.

"Aww, baby. That was very nice," Rosey said.

A red robin approached the window and started to chirp.

"God answered your prayer, baby."

Egypt was ecstatic. She had never witnessed a prayer answered so fast. Something was different about the bird's singing. Egypt actually understood what the little bird was chirping.

"I am a messenger from God. He sent me to let you know that he heard your prayer, and he is very pleased with you. He also told me to tell you that he will bless you with all the gifts that we, the Freedom Flyers, have."

"Freedom Flyers?" Egypt curiously asked. Rosey looked at Egypt.

"What, baby?" she asked.

"Oh, nothing, Grandma," she said nonchalantly. Rosey smiled and enjoyed the bird chirping.

Egypt and the robin stayed at the window, talking for a while. Rosey eventually took a nap from the peaceful robin's chirp.

Egypt remembered that she was supposed to help Aunt Beck go grocery shopping, so she ran back to the house. When she got there, Aunt Beck had already gone without her. When she went back outside, a red-tailed hawk was in a tree. Egypt was amazed at the beautiful feathers that the hawk possessed.

"A large storm is coming this summer. We will need shelter," the hawk said.

"You can stay on my aunt's porch. I'm sure she wouldn't mind."

"Thank you, but the porch is not big enough to house all of the birds in Beaufort."

Egypt looked around and wondered who could help her build a shelter for the birds. A small, white pickup truck slowly rolled down the dirt road.

"Uncle Two Thumb!" She yelled with excitement.

Egypt ran out of the house to her favorite uncle; the hawk flew to a nearby tree, where Uncle Two Thumb had parked. The hawk listened to Egypt as she talked to her uncle and built up the courage to inquire about building a shelter. Uncle Two Thumb glanced at the tree and saw the large bird about seven feet away from them.

"That's a red-tailed hawk! I've never seen one this close up!" Uncle Two Thumb said.

"Would you like to meet him?" Egypt asked.

"What do you mean meet him?"

"Yes, he's the one that asked for the shelter," Egypt confirmed.

"All right, let's meet him." Uncle Two Thumb decided to play along.

"My uncle would like to meet you. Can you please come down and meet him?" Egypt said while looking up in the tree.

The large hawk spread its wings and soared down to the hood of the truck! Uncle Two Thumb jumped back as the hawk's talons scratch the metal.

"Uncle Two Thumb, meet...what's your name?"

"Kreeear!" the hawk screamed.

"Rosh, meet Uncle Two Thumb!" Egypt said.

"So, you need a shelter by the summer. That gives me about ninety days. I will need some help to do it, but I'm sure I can get it done. What type of storm is happening this summer?" Uncle Two Thumb asked.

He watched as his favorite niece talked to a hawk.

"So, you can really understand what this bird is saying?" he asked.

Rosh spread his large wings and took flight into the sky.

"He's going to spread the word that Uncle Two Thumb is building the largest, most magnificent, most eye-catching shelter in all of Beaufort!" Egypt said, giving him a big hug."

"What up, Unc!" Brix yelled, entering through Aunt Beck's back porch, carrying two boxes.

"There you go," Egypt said, smiling at her uncle—as they both were thinking the same thing.

Uncle Two Thumb left for an hour. When he arrived, he had a trailer attached to his truck with a giant stack of lumber. A red flag was stapled to the end of the wood, trembling in the air. Brix and Egypt stood in the open land across from the library, and they guided the truck while Unc backed up. Doc came outside as he noticed the large amount of wood that Brix had unloaded and stacked up.

"What do y'all have going on?" Doc asked.

"Your granddaughter received a message from God. I was ordered to build a shelter for the birds; a storm is coming this summer," Uncle Two Thumb said with a small pencil behind his ear.

Doc glanced at Egypt and smiled; she returned the smile as Doc walked back into the house. Uncle Two Thumb and Brix worked on the bird shelter the entire day. The red-tailed hawk came soaring from above and landed near Egypt. He was accompanied by other birds.

"Hi, Rosh. Who are your friends?" Egypt asked.

"These are the Freedom Flyers," Rosh said proudly.

The birds all greeted Egypt and thanked her for her help. Brix looked at Rosh and admired his features, especially his eyes. Rosh and the Freedom Flyers did not stick around for long.

"Your uncle is doing a marvelous job. I will be back tomorrow; I just wanted the others to meet you and see where we will be sheltered."

Rosh and the other birds took flight into the open sky, and Egypt offered to get Uncle Two Thumb and Brix some food, but they were focused on building the foundation before darkness fell.

The two worked on the shelter day and night for two weeks straight. School resumed, and Egypt was back to finish the year before summer break. Every day after school, she would run to the shelter to see the progress that Uncle Two Thumb and Brix had made.

This particular day was a special day, as the shelter would be fully completed. Egypt got off the bus and noticed that she was able to see from a very far distance. She saw Brix and Uncle Two Thumb sitting outside of the shelter. When they saw the bus, they got up. Egypt ran to the shelter, leaving Dax and Breeze. When she arrived, Rosh was in a nearby tree, waiting for her. He flew down and gently landed on her shoulder, where she had made a custom patch for him to rest on.

"We were waiting for you to add the final touch," Uncle Two Thumb said.

"This is amazing! Can I go inside?" she asked.

Uncle Two Thumb stretched out his hand and walked Egypt inside. The shelter was beautiful; there were entry windows for a variety of birds. Bird feeders were in every corner and stacked to the top. Rosh flew to a corner with a tree branch and claimed his spot.

"There is one more thing that has to happen for it to be completed," Uncle Two Thumb said.

"What's that?" Egypt inquired.

"You have to give it a name."

"Freedom Flyers," She said, smiling at Rosh.

It was the last day of the school year, and Egypt was excited. She was ready for her summer break. She went outside to catch the bus and noticed several birds flying in a frenzy. The weather was beautiful, so she thought nothing of it, and she was eager for the last day of school. At the bus stop stood Breeze, Egypt, Dax, Fadez, and Bright. Everyone was excited for the last day of school. For most of them, this would be their last day attending middle school, and they all were looking forward to the summer break. The bus arrived, and they all got on. Egypt sat down in a vacant seat, and Dax sat next to her. Dax pulled out a notebook and pencil; he then started to write as the bus drove off. Egypt felt something sticking her under her arm.

"Aww!" she screamed, and she pulled a feather from under her arm.

Dax quickly turned his head when he saw the feather.

"What are you writing?" she asked, stuffing the feather into her pants pocket.

"Huh?"

"What are you writing?" She said as she quickly snatched the notebook out of his hand.

"Come on now! Stop playing before you rip it! Give it back!"

Egypt quietly read the letter.

"When I'm alone in my room, sometimes I stare at the wall. Is this LL Cool J's 'I Need Love?'" Egypt asked.

"Shhh!" Dax looked around, hoping no one had heard her.

Egypt tore the page out of the notebook and balled it up.

"What are you doing!" Dax yelled.

"Dax, you can't give her this! If you want to ask her out, you need to be original. Come on. I'll help you," Egypt said, turning to a clean sheet.

"My only question is, why would you wait for the end of the year to ask her out?"

"Because he's scary!" Breeze said while ease dropping from the seat behind them.

They quickly turned around and started laughing.

"No, I'm not!" Dax replied.

He took the notebook from Egypt and started writing down his own thoughts.

The school bell rang, and school was officially out for the summer. All the children in the class rushed out. Egypt took her time to enjoy the moment; this would be her last time as an eighth-grader. She was headed to high school in August. She slowly walked through the hall, fully embracing the smell of her transition from middle school. She continued her unbothered stroll through the hall and stopped before exiting outside. She looked up and saw a flock of birds flying south.

"A storm is coming!"

With her bird's eye view, hundreds of feet away, she saw Fadez and Shay talking. Shay blushed as Fadez charmed her with his unique game. Shay pulled out a flashy ink pin and held Fadez hand. Egypt focused in on Dax, with his hands clenching into a fist. Egypt looked up at the sky as the clouds transform from blue to gray! She looked at all of the students who had no clue what was about to take place. The peace of not knowing and the ignorance of not noticing the signs met head on!

The rain showered from the sky as the wind speed gained momentum! Egypt was attentive to the psithurism! The wind continued to howl as it passed through the school, shattering the windows. The destructive wind gust stretched an oak tree by its roots, and within seconds, the tree was uprooted from the earth. Catastrophic wind caused Egypt to run back into the school and take shelter. She ran into a corner near the girl's locker room and sat on the floor, covering her head. Egypt was frightened. The wind's wailing placed her in a state of trauma.

"Don't be frightened, my child. You are safe," a voice said to Egypt.

"Who's there? Hello! Is someone there?" Egypt asked.

"I am here with you, my child."

"God?" Egypt asked as she looked around.

"Yes, I am always with you. I have blessed you with dominion over every living creation that soars in the sky. Embrace your gifts and become familiar with the sky. Rosh will teach you everything you need to know about flying. He and Robin are my personal messengers. Thank you for honoring me and helping create a place to shelter their wings. Embrace your gifts."

Egypt slowly removed her hands from her head; the storm had passed. She looked through the busted window at the beautiful blue sky. The skin on her body gradually grew feathers. She waved her arms, and they turned into wings! She flapped her wings and began ascending from the ground.

"Embrace your gifts," God's voice reminded Egypt.

She took a deep breath and relaxed. When she exhaled, her entire body and being turned into a large bird. Egypt let go and let God; she trusted his words and remained calm.

"Egypt...Egypt."

Egypt didn't respond; she looked at Rosh and noticed that she resembled him.

"Come on. I have a lot to teach you."

Egypt jumped on the windowsill and chipped away the remaining glass so she could exit the window.

"Now just jump off and move your arms really fast. Once you take flight, you will get the hang of it."

Egypt jumped off the windowsill and moved her arms. Her body began ascending into the sky.

"I think I'm getting the hang of it!"

"Now, follow my lead. Move your arms up and down with grace. There you go; feel the air. Become one with it."

Mr. Bennett crouched down and picked up a feather from the ground. He watched Egypt as she flew away into the sky.

"Something is really interesting about this family. I will get to the bottom of it."

He placed the feather into a mason jar in his satchel and collected a blood sample that rested on a piece of the shattered window glass. He pulled out a cellular phone and began to dial.

"Hello, I found them. Yes, I'm sure."

A young Fadez gracefully swept the cut hair into a dustpan and placed it in a trash can.

"Hey, when you finish here, wipe down each station. Hey, keep y'all hands to yourself; control your little hormones! I can see everything that goes on," the owner of the shop said while looking at the camera in the corner.

Fadez and Shay both laughed.

"You know Dax really likes you. We got into a fight on the last day of school when we got home."

"Really, I'm sorry. Dax is cool, but he's not the one for me. You know my girl Sage has a crush on him. I mean, that's all she talks about. Dax this, Dax that," Shay said.

"Sage, I've noticed how she giggles and laugh at all his jokes. Maybe we should hook them up," Fadez said.

"You think he will talk to her?" Shay asked.

"Why don't you invite her to the movies with us tonight? I'll invite Dax," Fadez said.

"Great idea. Just don't tell him. It'll be like a blind date," Shay said.

They both finished cleaning the shop and headed outside. Three birds flew past them, almost grazing their faces.

"Wow! That was close!" Shay said.

One of the little birds circled back around and left the flock. The bird flew in Shay's direction before flying by Shay; white liquid was released from the bird. She looked up and was greeted with warm, runny, white and black waste. The waste oozed down her forehead to the side of her mouth.

"Get it off of me! Get it off!" she screamed.

Fadez took off his shirt and wiped the poop from her face.

"It is said, when a bird poops on you, it is considered good luck," he said, trying to calm her down.

Back at the bird shelter, Egypt and Dax were cleaning up and feeding the other birds. A little brown bird came by the window and started tweeting.

"Mission accomplished," Egypt told Dax as they both laughed hysterically.

Chapter 10:

THE FIERCE WARRIOR

Egypt lifted Brix from the ground, and they began to walk to the house. She noticed the gray residue on his shirt. Brix was weak. Whatever he was injected with had taken away his powers and strength. His legs gave out, and he fell to the ground.

"Get up! We have to get you in the house; they'll be back with more next time," Egypt said.

Brix pushed himself to the limit to make it to the front door of the Freedom Flyer. They enter through the front door and he fell on the floor. Egypt quickly ripped the shirt off of him. The gray residue started to affect her, and she instantly felt nauseous. She tossed the shirt out of the window.

"Brix! Stay with me! Don't close your eyes!"

Brix struggled to stay awake, but his strength was gone. A little exotic purple bird flew inside and landed on Egypt's shoulder; the purple bird started chirping.

"Yes, go find some help!" Egypt said as the little bird flew out the window.

"I remember when me and Unc built this place. It stood strong during that summer storm," Brix said as he coughed up mucus.

"You know we worked on this place from sunup to sundown. Unc didn't want to stop to eat or anything. He was determined," Brix said with a slight chuckle.

They both heard a noise toward the back of the shelter, where a little room held the supplies. Egypt quickly got up and drew the dagger from her ankle. A short man appeared. He wore a black robe that exposed his chiseled chest. His face was covered with a bushy dark beard. A dark brown, crown-shaped, pinched-front fedora with a three-inch brim sat perfectly on his head. His pants were three times the size of his waist, and his ankles were exposed from the pants being rolled up. His feet were bare.

"What y'all doing in yuh?" the man asked.

"Oh, it's just Uncle Glaze," Egypt said as she placed the dagger back into its holster. "Brix was attacked. We need to get him some help; he is getting weaker by the second."

Uncle Glaze face twisted in concern. He walked to Brix and knelt where he was. He lifted Brix up off the floor and helped him onto a sofa. The little bird flew back through the window, and Doc walked in moments afterward. He carried his staff and the chalice. Doc immediately went to Brix and held his face to the chalice.

"I tried my best to fight them off."

"Drink, my son; don't talk."

Glaze stood up; he was upset from what had happened to Brix.

"I wish I was here when it happened," he said with rage.

"Well…where were you?" Egypt asked.

"I was sleeping."

Brix drank from the chalice as Glaze and Egypt watched him. Doc looked to the window. His senses enhanced and tingled as he felt and heard someone approaching from another dimension.

"Take Brix into the back room until his strength and power are restored; they're back, with back up this time," he whispered.

"Who?" Glaze hissed.

"The soul seekers," Doc said.

Glaze went to a corner and retrieved a spear that hid behind a tall flowerpot.

"Daddy you stay right here. I got something for them."

Glaze removed his hat.

"Hold my hat."

"They have reinforcement with them!" Doc confirmed.

Egypt pulled out her Golden Dagger and readied herself for battle. Glaze walked to the door, and without warning, he kicked the door open! He ran outside and started engaging in battle. Egypt followed behind him and started fighting. Brix stretched his hand out, and his Zulu shield came soaring to his arm. He gripped the shield and felt his powers getting stronger. Doc gripped his staff and stood in front of him, and Brix gently walked to the side of Doc and directed him to get behind him. Doc gracefully moved.

The jet slowly descended and landed on the water; it then transformed into a submarine and went under the surface. The submarine sank to the bottom until it touched the ground. The submarine went into stealth mode. Breeze looked back, and everyone was looking at him for instructions.

"So, how are we going to get on the island from down here?" Myles asked.

"I have a friend that will assist us."

Breeze stood up and walked to the center of the submarine. He pulled down a ladder and opened the top. Everyone watched him as he manipulated the water from rushing in.

"Get your stuff and come out!"

Seven went first; he climbed up the ladder and stood on top of the submarine. He looked around as the water surrounded them in a small radius. Breeze's arms were spread out to control the water. Zaina followed Seven and stood on top. Blaze and Fadez followed after Zaina. Myles climbed the ladder, and Dax followed behind him. Staxx looked around the submarine for a second.

"Staxx. Staxx," a voice echoed in his head.

"It's me, Lauryn. Can you hear me?" Staxx stopped on the second ladder.

"Lauryn!"

"Yes! You're alive! I thought you were dead!" Staxx could hear the relief in Lauryn's voice.

"We are coming to get you. Just tell me where you are on the island."

Lauryn looked back and saw Soulek gaining on her. "I'm in a tunnel! Hurry!"

Staxx climbed up out of the submarine with the others.

"Lauryn! Lauryn!" he yelled. Their connection ended.

"She's here! She's in a tunnel," Staxx said, confused.

Breeze, still manipulating the water, whistled, and the sound waves rippled through the ocean.

"All right! On the count of three, I'm going to release my hold on the water, and I want you all to jump off of the submarine."

They all looked at him, in confusion.

"On three, I want you all to take a deep breath! Hold it and jump to your right! Y'all good?"

They all agreed, and Breeze slowly started counting.

"One...two...three!"

He lowered his arms, and the water rushed back in place! They all jumped off the submarine and landed on dolphins! Breeze didn't jump; he looked around to see if everyone was on a dolphin and led the way. The dolphins followed Breeze as he swam through the ocean with the speed of a sailfish. The Beings held on tight to the dolphins as they gracefully soared through the water. Breeze quickly took a left, and the nine dolphins followed him. Breeze arrived at the trail and quickly pulled himself onto the land. The dolphins waited for his signal; Breeze nodded his head, and the dolphins all gracefully jumped out of the water. The Beings held on! On their way down, the Beings jumped off the backs of the dolphins onto the trail.

"Lauryn said she was in a tunnel," Staxx whispered.

Breeze typed a few buttons into his wristwatch, and a small map of the island appeared.

"We are here. It looks like the tunnel is located here, above the cells. We all need to stay together. That's about a mile on foot," Breeze said.

"This island doesn't feel right. Let's get Lauryn and get out of here," Fadez said.

"It's too quiet on this island," Myles added.

The gray sky complimented the weary atmosphere that withered the flowers and bred the mold on the buildings. They all walked behind Night and Zaina. Crows crowed, and the privateness of the ocean grew anxious. The waves roared as if to alert the Beings' arrival.

Glaze and Egypt engaged in battle with the soul seekers. Glaze maneuvered with style and grace. He countered and attacked. His defense displayed impeccable speed. His feet moved as if he'd studied the great Muhammed Ali's movement. His fighting style was Jeet Kune Do, which had been created by the legendary Bruce Lee. Glaze moved like water, as his strikes were impulsive. His punches were vicious as he put his whole body into them! He moved with his hips and forced all of his energy from his body to his fist! Glaze's movements honorably conveyed him, which allowed his reflexes to be present when he needed them. He cleared the area! The soul seekers were no match for Glaze, the Geechie Warrior. One of the soul seekers reached for Glaze's spear, which he'd placed on the ground before engaging in battle. Egypt quickly threw her Golden Dagger at the soul seeker! The soul seeker dodged the dagger and caught it; he then picked up the spear and fled.

Egypt ran after him.

"I have to get that back!" she said while running after the soul seeker.

A portal activated, and the soul seeker ran inside! While running, Egypt transformed into a hawk and flew inside the portal behind the soul seeker. The portal closed, following Egypt's entrance. A rejuvenated Brix and raged Glaze walked through the soul seekers who were left on the ground. They groaned and moved with pain.

"Where Egypt?" Glaze asked.

"I don't know. I saw her running after one of them, and then she vanished."

"What do you mean, she vanished!" Glaze asked.

Brix crouched down and picked one of the soul seekers up half-way off the ground; he held him by his shirt. The soul seeker was in pain.

"Where is she?" Brix asked.

"The girl bird? Her feathers are being plucked one by one; then the girl bird will be lowered into a tub of boiling water in preparation for a feast. Just how your Gullah ancestors did."

Brix clenched his fist as he prepared to thrash the soul seeker's face into the ground. He was suddenly distracted by a bird's shriek!

"Egypt!" he exclaimed!

The soul seeker quickly drew a blade from his side and attempted to thrust it into Brix's flesh. Brix's magnetic force stopped the blade before it was inches from his heart. The soul seeker pushed with all of his vile and immoral energy! Brix glanced down at him and took the blade.

"You're not worth the muscle movement I will waste releasing you to hell," Brix said as he inserted the blade into the earth.

He stood up in search for Egypt. Glaze walked to the soul seeker and pulled the blade out of the ground.

"You're no match for the fierce warrior; your skills are novice compared to his," the soul seeker said before Glaze thrust the dagger in his neck.

"Egypt!" Brix yelled out. "Egypt!"

The bird's wailing increased and became louder. Brix clutched his shield and looked ahead. A large hole opened a short distance away from him. The hole was black with indistinct chatter chanting someone's arrival.

"What the—" Brix said as he prepared for what was coming out of the portal.

A large dark shadow slowly appeared on the ground. A shirtless, hairy man slowly walked. He held the hawk by its neck while its wings flapped! He stood over six feet tall, with ripped muscles. The hair on his head was nappy, thick, and black, connecting into a full beard. His skin was midnight dark with veins popping out of his body, clearly defining his strength and blood flow. His arms were immense and complimented his broad shoulders and vast shoulder blades. His brawny chest was plastered with nappy hair and well defined, three-dimensional. His core was sculpted with abdominal muscles that were also engulfed with nappy hair. His attire was camouflage pants with combat boots. One end of a nun chuck was securely tucked inside his waist band. A sharp metal shank, attached to the jukon-bu and kusari, dangled and clanked as he walked out of the portal onto the land. He looked around to admire his surroundings. He then held the hawk up and looked into its eyes. He tossed Egypt, and she landed beside Brix. She transformed back into her human form, coughing from the mammoth-sized hand that had suppressed her neck.

"Where you at, Glaze?" the man yelled out. "Glaze! Where you at?" His voice echoed through the trees.

"Are you going to be all right?" Brix asked Egypt.

"Yes, I will be ok. He has my Golden Dagger."

"Glaze! Where you at?" the man's voice indistinctly echoed feet away from them.

Brix stood up and gripped his shield; he slowly advanced toward the man. As he got closer, he couldn't help but notice the monstrous man that tolerated someone's delay. The portal closed, and Brix walked up to him with confidence in each step.

"Where's Gla—"

Brix connected his shield with the man's face. He followed with a devastating one-two punch to his midsection with his shield. The man pivoted back to regain his balance.

"That was solid," he said, slightly impressed.

Brix quickly grabbed the shield with both hands and swung at the man's head. The man back-stepped, pivoted, and completed a half circle, dodging the attack. With his back turned to Brix, he pivoted his waist with force! The nun chuck and shank swung and connected with Brix's thigh and opened his flesh. A large gash exposed his flesh, and blood quickly covered his white meat.

"This is the stench of flesh that Menelaus smelled when the prince of Troy's flesh was lacerated," the man said.

Brix placed pressure on his cut to try and stop the bleeding. He limped back on one leg to reengage in battle; the fierce warrior jumped into the air and cocked back his right fist. On his way down, his fist connected with Brix's face. Brix fell to the ground! The colossal man slowly walked to Brix, and Brix noticed the nun chuck swinging side to side. He quickly stretched his left hand out, and the nun chuck flew into his palm. The man looked befuddled! Brix stood up and limped toward the man, the pain from his leg slowing him down as the man quickly delivered a combination of strikes with his elbows and knees. Brix dropped the nun chuck and fell to the knee of his good leg.

"Stay down, boy," the man whispered to Brix.

He slowly stood up, his face smeared with the low country's dirt and his blood. Brix squared up with the man.

"My little sister hits harder than that," he said while spitting blood.

Brix swung and missed! He swung again; this time he leaned in! The man stepped back and grabbed Brix in a grapple. He pushed Brix off of him and followed with a knee to the midsection. The fierce warrior knelt down on one knee to time Brix's fall. Brix landed down on the knee of the man. Holding Brix with his left arm, he lifted and bent his elbow in the air and looked down at the back of Brix's head.

"Mungo!" a voice screamed out, alerting the man. He rolled Brix's body off of his knee and picked up his nun chuck.

"Yes, sah!" the man said as he turned around.

"You looking for me? I'm right cha!" Glaze announced.

Brix scooted back on his palms out the way. Mungo quickly picked up his nun chuck and walked toward Glaze. Glaze reached inside the pocket of his robe and ran toward Mungo. Mungo ran toward Glaze and began to swing his nun chuck to gain momentum! Glaze quickly pulled his hand out of his pocket. Mungo swung his nun chuck at Glaze, and Glaze rolled past him and squared up! Mungo turned around and was confronted with a punch from a gulf oyster drill shell to his eye!

"Ahhhhh!" Mungo screamed out as he held his eye.

Glaze pulled out another shell from his pocket and wore it as a brass knuckle. He delivered a one-two punch, wearing the shells on each fist. The punches opened up Mungo's face and allowed blood to leak out. Glaze took off his robe and slowly walked to Mungo. Mungo dropped to the ground and clenched a fist of dirt; as Glaze approached him, he tossed the dirt into Glaze's face! He quickly took his hands out of the shells and attempted to remove the dirt from his eyes. Mungo charged Glaze and attacked him with the nun chuck.

"Sheeo! Sheeo!"

The shank gracefully slid across his arm, followed by a fierce swipe across the face and an uppercut punch to the chin.

Glaze's body left his feet and landed on his back. A sliced-up Glaze lay helpless on the ground, covered in blood.

"I traveled all the way from another dimension to put you on your back. I must admit, it was truly worth the risk. I guess all those martial-art flicks didn't pay off. I told you I was coming back for you. Yeah, I got you now! It's time to meet your maker, Glaze!"

Mungo grabbed a hand full of Glaze's hair from the back. His hand instantly became wet from the activator. Mungo lifted Glaze by the back of his hair to deliver a death blow. Glaze quickly pulled a box cutter out of his back pocket and broke it off in Mungo's neck! Mungo dropped Glaze to the ground. The pain from the box cutter throbbed as Mungo panicked and attempted to remove the piece of metal. He fell to the ground and held his neck as the blood slowly leaked from his neck between his fingers. A portal opened, and two soul seekers ran toward Mungo; they quickly lifted him off the ground and carried him into the portal.

"Get off of me! Let me get him!" Mungo uttered.

The soul seekers entered the dark portal, and it vanished. Glaze stood up and followed the trail of blood that Mungo had left behind. Egypt and Brix walked and stood beside Glaze as he stooped down and rubbed the blood that was mixed in with the dirt.

"He'll be back," Glaze said as he picked up the broken piece of razor that had been in Mungo's neck.

Two ladies dressed in gold carefully wrapped Mungo's neck with a bandage. He sat in a large chair—fit for a king. The room was dark and gloomy, and his body was beaten and bruised from his encounter with Glaze. Behind him was a wall full of all types of weapons that were neatly arranged.

"You were not to engage in battle; you were sent there for two things," one of the Ladies said.

"Ahh," Mungo sighed as the other lady cleaned the cuts on his body.

"Did you get it?" Mungo asked.

"Yes, my Lord."

The soul seeker reached into his waistband and pulled out Egypt's Golden Dagger. He bowed his head as he handed it to Mungo. Mungo grasped the dagger and began to chuckle. His voiced echoed throughout the desolate room. In the shadowy corner stood the large angel with dark wings. He glared at the Golden Dagger from a distance, as chill bumps ran up his spine.

Chapter 11:

THE BREAKING OF THE BEINGZ

Lauryn took off her left glove and snapped her fingers. A small flame emerged and birthed light from the darkness. She looked behind and noticed that no one was following her.

"Why did you stop, my Queen?" Soulek asked.

"We have her right where we want her," Queen Dahlia said.

They watched as a small light at the end of the tunnel slowly diminished.

Soulek exhaled a deep breath that triggered the Queen.

"Your breath reeks of failure. Your lack of attentiveness has caused an uproar. You let the child slip through your hands one too many times. Your lethargic skills have not gone unnoticed. Your slothful energy has transferred onto the others. You have one more chance to prove you are worthy to be a leader. I should have killed you instead," Dahlia said, scowling at Soulek's burnt arm.

Soulek looked on as Dahlia gave him detailed orders. His failure bred resentment that ignited the fire of determination in him.

"Use the energy that you are currently feeling, let your failure and rage unite, and bring the souvenir back alive! Send word to the soul seekers to bring her back alive; enough of the cat and mouse games! I want her bowing down to me by sunrise!"

Queen Dahlia's beauty disguised her relentless approach to getting things done. She had a way with words. Soulek had never felt the wrath of Queen Dahlia until now. As she walked back, he walked in the opposite direction. He looked at his wounded arm and wrapped it in a piece of cloth. An angry Soulek walked through the tunnel, guided by determination and redemption.

"Reeks of failure. I am Soulek!"

His anguish grew by the second; he was focused on his mission, and nothing was going to stop him. Anything or anybody that came in his path would be annihilated.

The misty wind blew, owls hooted, crickets chirped, and the island was unwelcoming. Night slowly walked through the trail; leading the way, he stopped in his tracks.

"What's wrong?" Breeze asked.

Night didn't respond; he gestured them to stop by sticking his arm to the back with his hand open, revealing his palm. The Beings heard two voices chattering.

"Are you sure this is the way to the water?" the voice said.

"Yes! This is the way; I remember this trail that leads to the water," the other voice responded.

Two females dressed in hospital-patient gowns roamed the woods. They were barefoot in the dark. They both stopped running.

"I think we lost them. What's wrong?" one of the ladies asked.

She fell to the ground, overwhelmed with fatigue.

"Come on, Kiaya. We're almost there!"

"I can't move," she responded.

She reached and pulled a needle out of her lower back. They both looked at the large needle and half-full syringe of thick gray liquid. Kiaya dropped the syringe and started coughing, sweat pouring from her face. Her body cringed, and she felt shortness of breath and severe pain in her chest.

"I don't want to go out like this, Sue," Kiaya said.

"Girl, don't think like that; we are going to make it out of here alive. Look at me! Say it with me!"

"Alive!"

Two large bodies dropped feet away from the girls! With black metal stars engraved on the sides of their necks.

Zaina appeared out of the bushes and directed the girls to be quiet by placing her finger to her lips. Sue nodded her head, holding Kiaya in her arms. The Beings slowly appeared after Zaina.

Zaina crouched and assessed Kiaya.

"We have to get her out of here! Can you help us?" Sue asked.

Seven walked up, stooped down, and reached for the syringe. He thoroughly looked at it. Staxx crouched down with Seven to examine the needle. He quickly stepped back, as he felt lightheaded and dizzy. Seven saw the effect the syringe had on Staxx and gently pushed him back from it. Staxx immediately felt a relief from Seven's touch.

"What is that?" Staxx asked while rubbing the top of his bald head.

Dax walked over to the two guys. He gestured with his hands, and vines started rolling down a large tree. Dax and Blaze sat the two men against the large tree, and the vines began wrapping around them tightly. Blaze touched the vines with the tip of his index finger, and lightning shot up the vines.

"This should hold them," Blaze said.

"Are you able to talk?" Seven asked.

Kiaya looked up at Seven; she parted her cracked lips and tried to talk. Nothing came out of her mouth.

"Her muscles are deteriorating at a rapid pace," Seven said.

"The virus is working on her. This is a virus deadlier than the COVID-19, which plagued the world back in 2020. It spreads throughout the body and shuts down the organs and muscles within minutes. I can heal her, but I will need access to the submarine. Breeze! I will need your assistance. She doesn't have much time! We got to move quickly," Seven said, holding the syringe of gray liquid in one hand.

Seven pulled a black cloth out of his pocket and wrapped the syringe; he then placed the syringe into his backpack.

"Ok, we need to split up," Night said.

"Wait! What? Where are you taking her? I'm going with her!" Sue said.

"Wait! We need to know where you escaped from. We are searching for a friend; she said she was in a tunnel," Staxx said.

"All the girls are being held at the cell house. We managed to escape from the warden's house. This place enslaves women and young girls. My friend and I faked like we were ill. Once you take sick, they transfer you to the infirmary to get better," Sue explained.

"So, is this like some sort of sex-trafficking ring?" Fadez asked.

"Yes, they bring us onto the island, shackled neck, wrist, and feet. Once you enter the island, you are given several tests to see if you have any sorts of diseases."

"What happens if you have a disease?" Fadez inquired.

"You are quarantined for a minimum of fourteen days. Once you are well, you're placed back into the population. They have doctors and plastic surgeons who inject some of the ladies with enhancement shots to please certain customers. This place is hell on earth!" Sue said.

"So, the customers—are they brought to the island?" Myles asked.

"Most of the wealthy customers pull up on their yachts and handpick the girls for a weekend. The warden always sends security to protect his investments. The more discrete customers can order online, and the girls are shipped out to them with security. I've been here for over five years. I haven't had contact with my family since I was abducted from campus. Kiaya and I both—we were roommates. We were invited to a party on campus our second week of school. The drinks started flowing, and pills were taken. The next thing I recall, we were on a large boat in shackles with hundreds of girls from all over the world. We haven't had contact with our families since the day of the party," Sue said, rubbing Kiaya's head.

"She's burning up! Can you please help her?" Sue asked Seven.

"Seven, Breeze, and Myles, take them to safety so Seven can help Kiaya. Blaze, Fadez, Que, and Dax, head to the warden's house. Staxx, Zaina, and I will head to the cell house. We're not leaving this island until all the girls are safe," Night said, looking at Sue.

"There are guards throughout the island. Be safe," Sue said.

Breeze tapped on his wrist band, and the Beings received a notification on their bands.

"You all have access to the map of the island. Let's find Lauryn and shut this island down!"

Seven, Breeze, and Myles headed back to the submarine with the girls. Seven carried Kiaya in his arms as he followed Breeze. Myles walked behind Seven while Sue walked on the side of Seven. Kiaya opened her eyes and noticed the tall, silvered-haired, bearded man carrying her. She felt the fatigue leaving her body as Seven carried her. She touched his sleeve, which forced him to look down to her.

"Who, are you?" she whispered.

"A friend…a friend from God," Seven said.

Kiaya closed her eyes and let go all of her fears; she trusted that she was going to be taken care of. Her worries were no longer her burdens to bear. She held on to Seven tighter as her health strengthened.

Soulek came to the end of the tunnel and saw the ladder that led up to a manhole; the ladder had footprints on it. He slowly began to walk up the ladder; he stopped and looked around. The tunnel was dark, and the smell of feces and urine overwhelmed the small space. He jumped down from the ladder and landed on the ground. His boots were splashed with bodily waste. He reached down and grabbed a frock that was covered with excrement and urine, which gradually percolated through the drench fabrics. Soulek placed the frock on the ladder and resumed climbing up. He reached the top of the ladder and pushed up on the manhole cover and moved it to the side.

He climbed out of the tunnel onto the land. He looked over at the water. Soulek walked to the shallow water and noticed Lauryn swimming away! Lauryn glanced back and noticed Soulek walking in the water; she noticed that he was waist deep as his body slowly lowered into the water. His head was submerged. She resumed swimming as fast as she could; she swam the length of a football field nonstop. The water was still, and Lauryn stopped in the middle and treaded water. She looked around; there were no signs of Soulek. She gathered her breath and looked up into the sky…A bright light blinded her. The light slowly turned into a radiant bead of energy. The bead lowered from the sky and cast a beautiful indigo hue over the entire ocean. Lauryn looked around and became present in the moment. The awe-inspiring view soothed her soul as she stretched her arms up to receive the radiant indigo bead. The bead gracefully grasped the tips of her fingers. Suddenly, something gripped her ankles and yanked her under the surface. The bead slowly ascended back into the sky, the ocean darkened, and bubbles surfaced where Lauryn treaded.

Lauryn looked down and saw Soulek pulling her by the ankles! She tried to scream for help, but water rushed into her mouth and blocked her airway. She panicked as she was lowered deeper beneath the surface. She delivered a kick to his face that liberated one of her legs. She managed to swim back to the surface to get her head above the water for air! She then began to use her free leg to deliver more kicks, which exhausted her energy. Soulek regained his grip by pulling her thighs. Lauryn's arms moved rapidly as if she were climbing a ladder. Soulek delivered a forceful blow to the side of Lauryn's head. Her movement ceased, and her head was submerged back under the water, and her lungs were denied oxygen.

"Hypoxia. Hurry, my children! Lauryn needs your help!" Doc said.

The Beings all heard Doc's voice. Seven stopped in the shallow water before entering the submarine. He looked around; Myles did as well.

"What is hypoxia?" Myles asked.

"It's when you are deprived of adequate oxygen. In Lauryn case, I'm guessing it is dealing with drowning," Seven explained.

Soulek pulled a passed-out Lauryn by her legs to shore. He stood proudly as he picked her up and tossed her over onto his shoulder like a sack of potatoes. A group of soul seekers stood by and watched. They all stepped to the side as he walked through the crowd, holding Lauryn with one arm across his burnt shoulder.

"My Lord, let us bear the souvenir for you?"

"You hear that? They are offering their services to me! Reeks of failure are no longer associated with me. Your scrutiny that I've endured has birthed a new beginning! I am a worthy leader, a leader that will lead you all! From this day forward, refer to me as Lord Soulek!"

The soul seekers all bowed to Soulek. They stood back up and started cheering; one soul seeker approached and gave him a pair of metal gloves, gauntlets.

"My Lord, these will prevent her from using her powers—a gift from Lord Salvo The Fallen Angel," the soul seeker said as she placed the gloves on Lauryn, along with a double-looped metal handcuff cable.

The soul seekers hit their swords, causing a clanking sound to resonate throughout the island.

"Lord Soulek! Lord Soulek! Lord Soulek!" they cheered.

The Queen heard the loud chanting. She separated her curtains to get a view. A redeemed Soulek stood in the middle of a large crowd, with his followers chanting his name. Soulek looked up at the window.

"Is this what you want?"

Dahlia looked down at the crowd and indistinctly heard Soulek's voice over the chanting. She felt the shift in the position of power that she held over Soulek and her soldiers. The spirit of jealousy filled the vacancy where her soul once rested.

"He has gained their trust and loyalty. Bravo. He will never be equal to me," she said glaring through the window.

The windows opened, and the chanting ceased. Dahlia looked around at the large crowd that stood below her.

"Well done. Bring the souvenir to me, Lord Soulek," she said.

Lord Soulek's confidence increased as he gained validation from the only person, he'd pursued it from. The crowd kept chanting, "Lord Soulek! Lord Soulek!"

Lauryn started to cough, and water drained from her nose and gushed out of her mouth. She opened her eyes and noticed the large crowd cheering from a distance.

"Let me go!" she screamed.

"It's good for you to join me on our stroll."

"What do you want with me?"

"It has nothing to do with me—but everything to do with the universe conspiring. My destiny patiently waits. By morning, you will fully accept the inevitable," Soulek said.

Lauryn tried to escape, but Soulek's grip was too secure. She attempted to engage her powers, but the gloves prevented her from using the fire and ice.

"Your powers are not welcome here. The gloves that you are wearing are a custom pair made just for you, my dear. How do they fit? I know they're really snug; they were forged in a fire abyss as a gift from Lord Salvo The Fallen Angel, a master black smith from the Dark Realm. He only makes appearances on this pathetic planet when he is called by Queen Dahlia. Your fire and ice act was supremely impressive but inconvenient. The Queen sent word to The Fallen Angel to forge a gauntlet that will prevent any future acts from your hands, and he delivered in seconds. Now I will deliver you unto her as a token. My rise to prominence is evolving in the present moment. I have already succeeded as the next great leader of the soul seekers."

At this moment, Lauryn sensed a quarrel between the Queen and Soulek.

"Dahlia seems like a fierce leader that would not let someone like you next in line. You will never be leader as long as she sits on the throne," Lauryn added.

Soulek remained quiet while he deeply thought about the seed Lauryn had planted in his mind.

"Silence the alarm!" Soulek ordered as he approached the building.

The metal shields on the doors and windows slowly slid up, and he entered through the door. The red lights in the hall transitioned to a bright, clear light that illuminated the entire building. Soulek approached an elevator and entered. Two soul seekers were in the elevator.

"Where to, my Lord?" one of the soul seekers asked.

Soulek looked at him in disgust. The soul seeker nervously pressed a button on the elevator, closing the door and they began to move.

Lauryn closed her eyes and blocked out all the chatter and unwanted desires, and silence entered her mind.

Zaina, Night, and Staxx made it out of the trail and walked into an open area. The stillness raised the hairs on Night's arms. His senses tingled as he became fully alert. Night looked up into the sky, where the moon's light shined toward the east. Night tapped his band and looked at the map.

"We need to head here," he said.

He pointed to the moon, and Staxx and Zaina looked up. "The moon is guiding us to move east; the hospital is located in that direction."

"Wait, wait! It's Lauryn! She's in the...Golden Layer!" Staxx said.

Chapter 12:

THE GOLDEN LAYER

Zaina and Night both looked at Staxx.

"Lauryn! Lauryn!" Staxx yelled. "She's gone, again," Staxx said, feeling defeated.

"Golden Layer? Did she say anything else?" Night inquired.

"She was calm, very relaxed. It's like she had control over the situation.

"Seven, ask Sue where the Golden Layer is located on this island," Staxx whispered through his communication device.

Seven walked to the back of the submarine, where he bumped into Kiaya, who was cleaning herself. They both were caught by surprise. He tried not to stare at her as their eyes connected.

"I'm sorry. I didn't know you were getting dressed," Seven said sincerely.

"It's ok. You're not the first older man I got dressed in front of. Unfortunately, this island has forced me to do somethings that were against my will," Kiaya nonchalantly said while putting on a pair of yoga pants.

"Oh, your cousin Breeze has an extra pair of yoga pants that his lady friend left. He said she teaches yoga on the beach on the weekends." They both laughed.

"If you don't mind me asking, how old are you?" Kiaya inquired.

Seven rubbed his beard and chuckled.

"I'm twenty-four years old; the grey hairs can be a bit deceiving." They both laughed.

"I'm Seven, by the way," he said, extending his hand to shake hers.

Kiaya extended hers and softly grasped Seven's hand. She instantly felt a wave of energy rushing through her lower back.

"Wow! My back feels amazing," she confessed, while straightening. I've suffered from scoliosis for years. Seven—that's a really spiritual name. What's the significance behind it?" she asked.

"Perfection and completion. The number of power. My mom was in labor with me for six days, and on the seventh day, I arrived. When I was born, I had a head full of grey hair. My grandfather said it's because I will be a wise and noble man," he said, raising his index finger, imitating his grandfather.

They both laughed. Kiaya walked closer to Seven and rubbed his hand.

"Thank you for healing me earlier. I have never been in the presence of someone with so much grace and power. Well, was your grandfather, right?" she asked, shooting him a seductive glance.

Seven began to tell Kiaya about his grandfather and their mission.

Breeze and Sue walked into the room, and Kiaya slowly stepped away from Seven.

Seven looked at Breeze.

"My bad," Breeze's lips read.

Seven shook his head in laughter.

"No, it's all good," Seven said, making sure they knew there was nothing going on between him and Kiaya.

"Our friend is being held at the Golden Layer; can you tell us where that is on this map?" Seven asked Sue.

Sue looked at the map, confused. She zoomed in, and she zoomed out of the map.

"What's wrong? Breeze inquired.

"I know this island like the back of my hand. Not once have I noticed a Golden Layer. Trust me, if there were any gold on this island, me and my girl would have known. All right?" Sue said.

"Wait, there is a room!" Kiaya said, looking at Sue. "I followed two guards one night to the top floor of the hospital. They went in a room with a golden door. I hid outside of the room for hours; my curiosity got the best of me that night. A guard crept behind me and covered my mouth with a cloth. I squirmed and got a good look at him before passing out. All I remembered were red eyes. I never saw what was behind the door. When I woke up, I was in a small dark room."

"The hole," Sue said, as if she'd spent time there.

"I never said a word of that night until now," Kiaya said.

Dax, Que, Blaze, and Fadez arrived outside the gate to the warden's mansion.

"The runaway girl was right. Look at all the guards outside of the gated house. They are definitely protecting something," Blaze said.

"Yeah, this joint looks like Drake's embassy," Fadez said.

Dax shot Fadez a sideway look.

"Man! You ain't never step one foot on Drake's property," Dax said.

"I saw that Tootsie Slide video though," Fadez replied.

"Shhh!" Que said, nudging Fadez.

"Yo! Focus! We are about one hundred yards from the warden's crib. They have guards surrounding the place. Should we move in?" Blaze asked over his device.

"Nah, hold off a minute, Blaze. Not just yet. There's been a change in plans," Zaina said.

Dax squinted. His vision became enhanced, and he was able to see yards away through the gate into the warden's window. Dax blinked his eyes.

"Nah, this can't be right," he said.

"What do you see?" Fadez inquired.

Dax looked at Fadez.

"Who's there, Dax?" Que asked.

"Sticks and Stems," Dax answered.

"What? What are they doing here?" Fadez exclaimed.

Dax, Fadez, and Que started talking and planning how to move in.

"If we move in the front, we will alert the guards," Que said.

"I say we move in through the side; it's darker there and easier to move undetected," Dax said.

"Unc, what do you think? Unc? Wait!" Fadez yelled.

Blaze pulled the device from behind his ear and pulled out his bow. He quietly ran to the mansion. He climbed the ten-foot-tall metal gate and landed on a motion sensor that alerted the guards inside. The guards outside of the mansion all hurried through a secret entrance inside the gate. Fadez, Dax, and Que grabbed their weapons and headed to the mansion behind Blaze. Fadez engaged his speed and vanished from Que and Dax. He leaped over the gate! The guards and Blaze looked into the sky as Fadez came soaring down! He landed on his feet, his right fist punching the ground. They were cornered from every angle.

"Put down your weapon!" a guard yelled over an intercom.

Blaze's bow lit up with lightning, illuminating the entire yard.

"Shoot him!" one of the guards yelled.

Fadez jumped in front of Blaze and hugged him. Several shots went off from the inside of the gate. Staxx, Zaina, and Night looked in the direction where they'd heard the rounds of ammo.

"They're in trouble!" Myles said as he hurried to the ladder of the submarine.

"Breeze, let me out!" Myles said.

"We are about eighty feet underwater, cuz. I don't think that would be a good idea," Breeze said.

Myles grabbed his two axes and teleported out of the submarine, leaving a trail of purple fog. Breeze, Seven, Kiaya, and Sue all looked at the fog in astonishment.

"No, honey! Let's go! Did you see what he did? He disappeared! Like a ghost, girl!" Sue said dramatically.

"Sue, Sue, calm down. They were sent here by God. They're Supreme Beings," Kiaya said while looking at Seven.

"Child, this old man done got in your head. If you say so, I guess," Sue said as she sat down in a chair, patting her head.

Myles's vision became tunneled as he teleported through the water. On his flank were two dolphins, and they moved at light speed and made clicking sounds. The two dolphins guided him through the water as they approached the land. Myles appeared. He rubbed his clothes to see if he was wet, but they were dry. The two dolphins leaped out of the water and gestured their flippers up and down. They landed and began to utter pulses.

"Thank you," Myles said as the dolphins submerged.

Que dropped to the ground. Dax quickly took a knee and pulled out his bow and arrow. His sharp-shooting skills engaged as he focused on the guards. The guards started falling down one by one. Blaze looked back and noticed a black arrow soaring in his direction. He ducked, and the arrow pierced one of the guards a few feet away from him. More guards came out of the house as a guiding light circle the island. Blaze laid Fadez down; his body was filled with holes from the bullets that he'd taken.

"Why did you do that?" Blaze asked.

Fadez inhaled deeply and closed his eyes. He didn't respond to Blaze; he just continued to breathe deeply. The bullets slowly started popping out of his flesh as the wounds healed. Fadez slowly sat up with the help of Blaze.

"You gotta stop running off like that, Unc," Fadez said.

Three arrows pierced three guards as Dax and Que came across the gate. Blaze stood up and pulled Fadez up with him. He gripped his bow, and it extended. Que pulled out his dagger, and they all began to engage in battle. Dax sniped the guards that stood on top of the light house, about a half a mile away. Fadez and Blaze headed inside the warden's mansion. Dax continued to take down the guards with his arrows from a distance. Que maneuvered with the flaming sword and branded the guards with every swing. One guard grabbed Que from behind. Que didn't budge; he quickly placed his sword back into the holster and clenched his fists. His entire upper body began to ignite with a blue flame! The guard quickly released Que as the flame engulfed him.

"Help! Help!" the guard screamed franticly as the fire burned through his clothes. Dax reached to the sky and yanked his arm down with force. Rain showered down, directed at the burning guard, and instantly put out the fire.

"We didn't come here to set people on fire. Let's move," Dax said.

Que didn't respond. For a minute, it seemed like he'd blacked out.

"I lost control of myself for a minute," he said.

"Can you guys hear me?" Seven asked.

"Yes, we can hear you," Night confirmed.

"The virus that was injected into Kiaya is airborne. Make sure to cover your mouth and nose; this is a lethal virus! It will attack your inner body in seconds if you inhale the deadly toxins," Seven said.

"Attached to your holster is a face guard that protects you from extreme weather and toxins. Put those on," Breeze said.

The Beings all reached into their holsters and found the face guards. The shooting had ceased. Zaina, Night, and Staxx proceeded to the hospital. Zaina and Staxx looked at Night for directions.

"What's the plan, Night?" Staxx inquired.

Night looked around. The bright lighthouse light slowly moved toward the hospital and illuminated its windows.

"Get down!" Staxx exclaimed.

They got down, and the light shined on the hospital. Night looked up and saw an entrance to a window on the top floor.

"We go through that window." He pointed up.

"We need to make it inside before the light circles back around," Night confirmed.

"Follow me!" Zaina said.

She pulled her hood over her head and took three steps back before running and climbing up the wall of the hospital. She pulled herself up to look through the first window. Inside were empty hospital beds raised at an acute angle. The room was empty and seemed like it hadn't been used in years.

"What do you see?" Night asked.

"A few beds. Other than that, it's empty."

Zaina continued to climb to the next room. She looked through the window and saw someone passing through the room, wearing a hazard outfit. The person backtracked and headed toward the window. Zaina heard the footsteps getting closer. She slowly pulled out her mini sword, and the window opened. She heard deep breathing in the bio mask. She gripped her sword tighter with one hand and held onto a brick that poked out of the wall with the other. As the window opened, the masked person looked out. Night took off his shades and looked up, and a dark shadow came from his eyes, camouflaging Zaina. The shadow was extremely dark, the person hurried back into the window and locked it.

"Where are you? We need you on the third floor."

"I'm headed there now. I thought I saw something outside. It probably was a crow or something."

Zaina signaled Night and Staxx to climb up the brick wall. Night placed his glasses back on, and the dark shadow diminished, and they started to climb the wall. Staxx followed behind him. Once they'd all made it inside the window to the hospital, Night informed the others.

"We made it into the hospital," Night said through his device.

"Look for a golden door on the top floor," Seven said.

"Blaze and I are in the warden's mansion. Yeah, his money is long. I'm talking heated marble floors and all," Fadez said.

"How are all the girls going to fit in this submarine?" Sue inquired.

"How many girls are on the island?" Seven asked.

"Thousands, not including the girls that's scheduled to be shipped back. They are all at the cell house," she added.

Seven walked over to Breeze, who was viewing the map.

"Hey, we have a problem. There are more than a thousand girls on this island. We don't have the capacity to fit all the girls in here. You think you can get more of your marine mammal friends to help us?" Seven asked.

Blaze and Fadez slowly walked through the warden's mansion while Dax and Que remained outside. They heard fumbling in a room down the hall and slowly walked to the room.

The door flew open, and three men ran out. Sticks, Stems, and a middle-aged white guy. He wore a grey suit with hard-bottom shoes. He held on tightly to a briefcase as he ran. Sticks and Stems turned around and started shooting at Blaze and Fadez. They quickly jumped into a room in the hall and landed on the floor.

"That's got to be the warden they're protecting," Blaze said.

"Yeah, I wonder what's in that briefcase? You saw how he was holding it?" Fadez inquired.

"Ok, I'm going after the warden; you take care of your boys," Blaze said.

"Let me go first." Fadez said, standing up and walking back to the door. He poked his head out, and bullets came soaring at him. He dodged the bullets and ran up the wall. Sticks and Stems let off several rounds, trying to hit the moving target. Fadez quickly ran to the other side of the hall and sped up the ceiling. Sticks and Stems looked up, and no one there. They turned around, and Fadez was holding their guns.

"Fadez?" they said in unison.

"Get in the room!" Fadez said aggressively.

Fadez nodded at Blaze. He then went after the warden. Blaze walked through the mansion, searching every nook and cranny for the warden. He came across an open door that led into a room. Blaze heard a man whispering beyond the door. He slowly crept into the room and saw the same man that had run out of the room with Sticks and Stems. The man turned around quickly from the sound of crackling electricity. He picked the briefcase up off the floor and pulled a .38 revolver from his waist.

"Stay back! I'm not afraid to use this!" he exclaimed.

Blaze slowly raised his arms to show the man he was unarmed.

"What's in the briefcase?" Blaze inquired.

"You're not qualified to question me. I'll do the questioning."

"My bad, playa!" Blaze said.

"What are you doing on my island, and how did you get here?"

So, he is the warden, Blaze thought to himself.

"To keep it a buck, I'm just looking for a friend. We got word that she was here, so when I find her, I will leave your island. What kind of operation are you running here anyway?" Blaze asked.

The warden cocked his gun to show that he was serious.

"I will shoot you in your face!" he said.

He looked up at the light that was flickering. Blaze quickly pulled out his bow and knocked the gun out of the warden's hand. The gun went off as it hit the floor. Blaze extended the bow and delivered an electric one-two hit to the warden's head and arm. The warden dropped the briefcase, and Blaze picked it up off the ground.

"What do you have in here?" Blaze asked.

"Don't open it!" the warden yelled out.

Blaze opened the briefcase. Inside were tubes filled with blood samples and pictures of girls.

Blaze skimmed through the pictures and the tubes. One picture, in particular, triggered him. Blaze pulled the picture out of the briefcase and dropped it. The tubes of blood clinked as they hit one another.

"What are you doing with her photo?"

He yanked the warden by his shirt and tie.

"Where is she?" Blaze inquired, showing the warden the picture.

"Who's that?" the warden stammered.

"Where is she?" Blaze repeated, shoving the picture into the warden's face.

The warden began to stammer and squirm. Blaze mistakenly dropped the picture; it slowly fluttered to the ground.

"Ahhhhh!" The warden screamed as the electrical current passed through Blaze's hand and began to electrocute him.

"Ok!" the warden exclaimed.

A low-frequency energy suddenly filled the room as the lights went out. Blaze released his grip on the warden. His shirt collar was burnt with black, and ashes smeared his white button-up shirt. His tie hung halfway off of his neck, which exposed his third-degree burn marks. A large, dark opening appeared on the opposite side of the large room. Energy circled the opening, illuminating the room. Mungo slowly walked out of the portal and looked around. His appearance demanded Blaze's and the warden's attention. His fresh wounds, which Glaze had blessed him with, turned the white bandages into a merlot hue. Inside his waistband was Egypt's golden dagger; on the other side of his belt was his infamous nun chuck with the dangling shank.

"You must be Blaze," he said as the portal closed behind him.

Blaze squared up.

"Yeah, I am Blaze. Who are you?" Blaze asked. The warden slowly moved out of the way and picked up his briefcase.

"Your brother found who I am through blood, sweat, and tears."

Blaze removed his bow, enabling it to extend.

"Nice, nice. The name is Mungo, a weapon connoisseur," he said, gazing at the bow. "After I thrash you, I will take your little light pole and hang it up on my wall, along with all the other souvenirs I collected from nonentities such as yourself."

Blaze sized Mungo up to calculate how much voltage it would take to bring him down. He held the bow with both hands to increase the voltage. The electric charge gained momentum, and the current rapidly moved from his body onto his bow. Mungo started walking toward Blaze, unbothered by the electricity.

"You know, traveling to earth twice in a day has really raised my stock. Your brother has heart, I must admit, but he is still wet behind the ears. The young man's skills are the skills of a novice," Mungo said.

The rumbling sounds of thunder filled the room as Blaze sent a thunderous slap to Mungo's face from his bow. The electrical impact sent Mungo flying out of the room, and his body shook helplessly on the ground. Blaze, full of rage, walked out into the hallway and saw Mungo slowly getting back up.

"What's that about a million volts and an amp? You trying to take me out here, boy?" Mungo asked as he brushed the burnt hair off of his chest.

"What did you do to my brother?"

Mungo rubbed the bandage on his neck and looked at his fingers. The wound on his neck had reopened.

"I'm going to make this one quick, as a matter of fact. Give me the bow, and I'll leave in peace," Mungo said as the portal reopened.

Blaze stepped to the side to get a look into the portal, where the electric current fluctuated.

"Yeah, you got me messed up, for sure," Blaze said as he charged the bow with lightning.

Mungo pulled his nun chuck out and began to swing it around in the air. The warden gathered all of his belongings and carefully crawled to a door that led to another room. Blaze noticed the warden crawling; he immediately sent a wave of electricity that trapped the warden's arms against his side and torso.

"Where do you think you're going? I'm not done with you yet," Blaze said as the warden groaned in agony.

Mungo smiled as the nun chuck continued to gain momentum, swinging through the air by the handle. Blaze charged Mungo and began to engage in battle. Mungo swung the nun chuck shank at Blaze's head. Blaze held out his bow, gripping it with both hands. The chain swiftly wrapped around the middle of the bow. Blaze tried to pull himself away, but Mungo's strength was too much.

"You're sadly mistaken if you think you can overpower me! I have the strength of ten silverback gorillas!" Mungo said.

Blaze's eyeballs turned from white into a Carolina blue, with horizontal lightning. Blaze's hands glowed with lightning as he manipulated all of the electricity on the island. All the lights turned off as Blaze absorbed the electrical energy! Mungo released his grip and it sent electrical shock waves through his body. The nun chuck turned blue from having contact with the electric bow. Mungo stepped back and looked at his hands as he tried to shake the paralyzing shock off. Blaze placed his bow in the holster on his back and picked up the nun chuck. The electricity crackled as Blaze grasped the nun chuck. Mungo, still shaken from the shock, was unable to move. Blaze swung the nun chuck and connected with Mungo's midsection, gashing his abdomen. The nun chuck hit the floor, and two vicious lightning bolts shattered the windows and struck Mungo in the back. The thunder roared as Mungo fell to the ground and cracked the marble floor. A charged-up Blaze walked slowly and stood over Mungo's body; he raised his arms up and lets out a furious scream.

Lightning came soaring from all angles onto Blaze's body. Mungo's eyes slowly opened. The warden maneuvered his hand out of the electrical restraint and retrieved a gun.

Two shots struck Blaze's back... bringing him to his knees. Blaze's electrical powers declined at a rapid pace, and he reached into his back and attempted to pull out a needle. The syringe was filled with grayish liquid. He fell on his face, shaking uncontrollably. Mungo regained enough strength to crawl over to Blaze, and he noticed two syringes bulging out in Blaze's back.

"The Zun Serum." Mungo said while pushing down on the needles, injecting the grayish liquid into Blaze's spine, afflicting him with pain.

"Awwwww!" Blaze screamed before passing out.

Mungo stood up in agony, applying pressure to his abdomen. He looked down at the bow, which was securely placed in its holster. He reached down with one hand and ripped the holster off of Blaze's back. He took the bow out of the holster to examine it.

"Mmmm. This will add value to my collection."

Mungo turned to the portal and began to walk in.

"Hey! Help me! I saved you! Get me out of here," the warden yelled out.

Mungo turned around and looked at the warden, still holding the gun that brought Blaze down.

"Drop the gun," Mungo insisted.

The warden released the gun, and Mungo picked it up and placed Blaze's bow down.

"Fool," he said as he began to walk back toward the portal.

"I saved your life!" the warden yelled.

Mungo looked down and noticed a picture. He placed the gun in his waistband and picked the picture up off of the ground.

"The girl bird," he chuckled.

"Do you know her?" the warden inquired.

"What value is she to you?" Mungo inquired.

The warden took the opportunity to engage in a conversation with Mungo.

"Let me out of here, and I can show you her value. I've been searching for her for years."

Mungo walked over to the warden and ripped the electrical wrap off of him.

"Thank you, Mungo it is?"

"Yes, Mungo. Now tell me about the girl bird," Mungo said.

"Do you know where she is?" the warden inquired.

"Of course, I do. Why?"

"Egypt is a very special girl. She has the ability to transform into a hawk! I saw it with my own eyes. Obtaining enough of her blood will allow me to breed new life," the warden said.

"What are you? Some sort of freak?" Mungo asked.

"Freak? No. Creator? Yes! I've observed that you have a great taste in weaponry," the warden said.

That seized Mungo's attention.

"Follow me. I may have something that interests you."

Mungo followed the warden into a secret closet in the large room.

"Watch your head," the warden said as he entered the room.

Mungo lowered his head and entered the large closet.

"First, you have to tell me where I can find Egypt," the warden demanded.

"She was last seen in the Carolinas. South Carolina, to be exact. I can still feel her ruffled feathers in my palm as she wailed for help. She is protected by her cousin and her uncle. Capturing her will not be a walk in the park," Mungo said while exposing his wounds from Glaze.

The warden exhaled deeply and began to retrieve a large briefcase from the corner.

"Tell me what you think about this," the warden said while handing the heavy briefcase to Mungo.

Mungo opened the brief case and pulled out a war hammer. The heavy briefcase dropped to the floor as Mungo placed all of his attention on the gold war hammer.

"Help me capture Egypt and her family, and I will make sure you obtain every war piece that was ever created," the warden said.

"Your offer is delightful. I am in no shape to take on Glaze and his nephew. However, I have a personal vendetta with that family that needs to be resolved. I would gain much satisfaction watching them die slow from a strike," Mungo said while rubbing the war hammer.

"Here, I will not be needing this. There is no value in a gun. Slashing and cutting flesh is a work of art," Mungo said while handing the gun to the warden.

"There is some unfinished business I have to handle. Give me a day, and I will bring each family member to you in chains and shackles," Mungo said while sticking out his hand to seal the deal.

The warden shook Mungo's hand, sealing the deal.

Chapter 13:

GOD IS MY STRENGTH.

At the hospital, Zaina, Night, and Staxx made it through the window to the top floor. The room they entered was dark, and the walls were painted black. Night took off his shades, and a bright light emerged from his eyes, giving light to the dark room. Night looked around, and the room didn't have much in it. Zaina and Staxx followed his lead as he walked to a door. Night turned the knob on the door and opened the door. He blinked his eyes, and the bright light faded out. Night placed his dark shades back over his eyes and slowly stepped out of the room.

"I see the golden door," he whispered to Zaina and Staxx.

"Two guards are guarding the door."

The two guards held their assault rifles with their fingers on the triggers. Zaina calmly pulled her hoodie over her head and walked into the hall. She pulled out two black stars and threw them at the guards.

"Hey! Hold it right!" one of the guards yelled.

Zaina continued to walk, and both of the guards touched their necks and fell to the floor.

"This will keep them down temporarily," Zaina said.

Staxx and Night took the guns and tied the men up with their backs touching. Zaina turned the doorknob to the golden door, and it was locked. She pulled a bobby pin out of her hair and placed it inside the keyhole. She began to move it around. There was a click, and Zaina pulled the pin out of the keyhole. She turned the knob and slowly began to open the door.

Myles arrived outside of the mansion and was confronted by the large gate. He looked on the ground and saw the communication device that Breeze had given them. He picked up the device and placed it in his pocket. He quickly teleported to the side of the gate; bodies were scattered across the lawn. There were no signs of Que, Blaze, Dax, or Fadez, except for the arrows that had pierced the guards.

"Yo. Where are you guys? I'm walking up to the front door of the mansion. I'm heading in," Myles said.

The silence answered back. He walked into the large mansion and saw a flickering light down the hall.

"Blaze!" Myles said as he ran down the hall. "Blaze!" he continued to yell.

Myles stopped running as he got closer and noticed the large hole with electricity circulating around it. He was lost for words. He glanced over and saw Blaze on his stomach.

"What the…Blaze!" Myles shouted as he walked over to him.

He saw the needles buried in his back.

"Hang in there, cuz. I got you," Myles said as he slowly pulled the needles out of Blaze's back.

Fadez, Que, and Dax appeared on the scene. Fadez stopped in his tracks, tears pouring down his face as he thought of the worst outcome. Que and Dax helped Myles pick Blaze up off of the floor.

"Is he?" Fadez asked.

Myles looked at Fadez. His facial expression spoke a thousand words. Tears fell down his face as he held onto Blaze. They all looked at the portal, which continued to crackle with electricity. Myles thought back to the moment he'd received his gift from God; he remembered the light and the message that came with it. He made a circle with his hands and placed his hand below his chest; a circular light appeared in Myles's hands. Que, Dax, and Fadez looked at the light as Myles held it in the palm of his hand.

"Whoever did this to Blaze came out of this portal. I'm going in to find him," Myles said, wiping the tears from his eyes.

"I am too," Fadez replied.

"This light will guide us," Myles said.

"I don't know about this; it could be a trap. Look at Blaze," Que said.

"I just have to find out for myself," Myles replied.

"Que and I will take Blaze back to the submarine," Dax said.

Fadez slowly nodded his head at Dax and Que.

"We'll be back," Que confirmed.

Dax and Que left the room, carrying Blaze.

"What happened to Sticks and Stems?" Dax asked.

Fadez reached into his back pocket and pulled two oddly shaped keys and what seemed to be a key card.

"They had these on them. They wouldn't say what it was for, but they were willing to lose their lives over it," Fadez said.

Dax walked over to Fadez to retrieve the key cards. Dax hugged Fadez, whispering in his ear. Dax slowly pulled back; he looked Fadez in the eyes.

"Are you sure?" Dax asked.

"Yes. I'm sure," Fadez replied.

Zaina slowly opened the door, and Night pulled out his crescent moon knives. Staxx felt a force in the room, and he immediately pulled the door shut! They all backed up from the door as a loud thumping came from the inside of the room.

"What is that?" Zaina asked.

Staxx closed his eyes and walked to the door.

"What are you doing?" Night asked.

Staxx touched the door. He felt whoever or whatever it was calming down and touched the door from the other side; their energies connected!

"Help…me," a voice on the other side of the door desperately said.

Staxx quickly opened his eyes and opened the door. A lady fell into his arms, and he quickly stepped inside of the room. Zaina and Night followed. Staxx laid her on the floor.

"What have they done to you?" he asked.

"If we walk through this portal, there is a chance that we may not make it back," Fadez said to Myles.

"Don't think negatively. We will find what we are looking for; we have the gifts," Myles said, opening his hands, showing the ball of energy that gleamed.

"Let me quarterback this. With your speed and my guiding light, we will walk through this portal. The light will guide us. Trust me," Myles said.

Fadez picked Blaze's bow up off of the ground and placed it in his waistband.

Fadez and Myles grabbed each other's hands, and both took the first step of faith.

Que and Dax arrived at the edge of the water; the submarine emerged.

Breeze climbed out of the top and helped Blaze inside. Seven saw Blaze and immediately went to him.

"He's been injected with the virus. Looks like a triple dosage."

Seven opened both of his hands, revealing his palms. He began to glow with a cosmic energy; he placed both of his hand on Blaze's back, where he'd been injected. The orange energy slowly traveled through Blaze's body. Seven began to breathe heavily as his energy increased and more transferred into Blaze's body. Everyone looked on and witnessed Seven's power.

"Everyone, stand back!" Seven ordered.

A crisp lightning bolt cracked through the titanium, breaching the hulls. Another bolt followed, striking Blaze in the chest. His body left the floor, causing the electricity to subsume his body.

The submarine started to shake as waves sucked it into the current. It rocked back and forth, causing everyone to hold onto a pole or ladder that led to the exit. Water began to leak inside of the submarine, but Seven was unbothered. His eyes transitioned into electricity as Breeze and the others watched.

"We have to get out of here!" Que said to Dax.

Sue and Kiaya both held on for dear life as the water began to rise inside the submarine. Breeze looked up and felt a large wave approaching. Before he could hold up his hands, the wave rushed the submarine, tossing it around like a pebble skipping on water. Water infiltrated the sub; Breeze swam through the sub to get a head count. The sub quickly began to submerge until it touched the bottom of the ocean. "Thump!" The loud sound of the titanium submarine alerted the fish, and they all scattered out of the way. As the sand settled, Breeze opened the top of the sub, and he began to pulse and send sound waves throughout the ocean. He swam back inside to Sue and Kiaya. He found them in the back of the sub, holding onto each other. He placed his hand on their lungs, and they both gasped. Their eyes opened, and they began to panic. He held out his hands, which glowed with purple rays of energy. They both grabbed each hand. Breeze quickly soared to the top of the sub, exiting with speed. Outside of the sub were the same dolphins that had helped them. Dax and Que followed Breeze. Sue and Kiaya held onto the dolphins as they swam to the surface of the ocean. Que and Dax began to swim. Breeze swam back inside of the sub to assist Seven and Blaze. Inside the shipwrecked submarine, Seven pressed firmly on the middle of Blaze's chest. Seven took a deep breath as his fist glowed yellow. The entire ocean lit up from his fist—a golden hue. He pressed hard on Blaze's chest; Blaze's body jerked significantly from the power! His eyes opened wide. Blaze raised his hand up to the sky, and a lightning bolt came soaring through the ocean. Blaze caught the bolt, while holding onto Seven. The lightning bolt carried them out of the ocean.

Dax and Que were both blinded by a bright yellow light. They stopped and treaded the water.

Once the yellow light had diminished, the dark ocean returned. Dax looked behind himself and saw a great white shark approaching. He hit Que to alert him. Dax and Que began to swim faster, but they were too late.

The room was extremely cold, and the aroma of blood saturated the air. Zaina flipped a light switch. She looked around the room. A hospital bed sat upright with brown leather straps dangling, as if someone had just broken free. Tubes and a ventilator were nearby the bed. Night placed his knives back into his holster and assessed the person with Staxx. A needle hung from the crest of her arm, where her forearm and bicep connected. Her wrist was discolored from what seemed to be a tight restraint. Her hospital gown was drenched in urine from the waist down. Staxx lifted her left wrist and read a band with several numbers. Staxx touched her forehead and closed his eyes.

"Who are you?" His thoughts traveled to the young girl's mind.

"Ivy," she responded.

"Who did this to you?"

"The warden."

Staxx read Ivy's energy; she was trying to channel a low-frequency energy. He hovered his hand over her body to examine it for any injuries, external and internal. Ivy appeared healthy physically, but her psyche was damaged. Mentally, she was stressed, scared, traumatized, and insecure. Anxious thoughts fluttered around her mind. He pulled a needle out of her arm and saw that it was filled with white liquid. Staxx thought back to Kiaya and the syringe. He ejected three drips of the liquid on his finger. There was a negative response to the liquid.

"This is a placebo."

The shark's mouth opened, exposing its razor-sharp teeth! Que sent a fury of fire balls in the shark's direction. The large shark propelled itself through the water, unable to move out the way of the fireballs. It positioned its fins to manipulate the water. The fireballs curved, missing the shark. The shark grew angry. Que quickly sent more fireballs at the shark, and again, the shark used his fins to create a distraction with the water. Dax summoned a sand tornado from the bottom of the ocean, causing a whirlwind in the ocean. They both took that time to swim away from the fifteen-foot killer. The moon shined on top of the water as Dax and Que got closer to the surface. The pressure at the bottom of the ocean grew, which caused them to look down. The shark had resurfaced and was coming back toward them! They both swam toward the shore; the shark began to move its tail back and forth and suddenly gained momentum.

The shark's mouth opened again, and his lower jaw revealed his meat-slashing teeth, and his head moved back to reveal the top layer of teeth. He went in for the kill, opening for Que! Que glanced at the layers of teeth in the shark's mouth; there were layers on top of layers. The shark slowed down and quickly flapped its tail, moving 180 degrees. The shark flapped its tail again, swinging Breeze off of him! Breeze gained his composure, while the shark, without hesitation, went after him. Breeze quickly signaled Dax and Que to get out of the water as he waited patiently for the killer. The shark's fins moved quickly up and down, which made him soar through the water. Breeze took off his necklace with the black diamond pendant and held it in the palm of his hand.

Breeze fled from the shark, swimming for the bottom of the ocean. A trail of bubbles lingered behind Breeze as the shark struggled to keep up with him. Breeze began to pray.

"God, please grant me the power and the strength that you blessed Moses with."

Breeze made it to the bottom of the ocean, and his feet planted in the sand, marking his footprints. Breeze stood at the bottom of the ocean and waited for the shark. The large shark caused turbulence in the ocean by flapping his monstrous tail through the water, breeding tidal waves. The shark's speed increased, the closer he got to Breeze. Breeze tried communicating with the shark to stop him from approaching. The shark rejected Breeze's thoughts and opened his mouth to inflict damage. Breeze quickly knelt down and punched the earth with the black pendant in his fist.

The water parted to the left and to the right, soaring into the sky. Breeze continued to kneel, with his fist embedded in the earth. The ground was dry as the desert's sand. The pendant was buried in the earth. The oversized shark leaped up and down on the floor of the ocean; his desire for water was essential as he bounced to the left, seeing the ocean from the side.

Breeze opened his eyes and looked to his left; a beautiful aquarium of fish, sea turtles, and exotic animals swam freely up to the sky. He looked at the large shark in front of him, gasping for life, his tar-colored eyes revealing that he was slipping away. Breeze then looked up. The ocean's surface stood hundreds of feet in the sky. His path was clear. It led to the island. He jumped over the shark and started running back to the island. Dax, Que, Seven, Blaze, and the girls all looked up at the ocean in the sky. They were all in awe. Kiaya started crying. Their eyes had never seen such a Godly view. The ocean ascended into the sky, like a reverse waterfall. The water remained parted as Breeze walked down the clear path, his fist glowing with a royal hue. A subtle voice whispered to him, "I am always with you. I am your strength."

Chapter 14:

TRUST THE JOURNEY.

"This island is corrupted. Where did you say the other girls were?" Blaze asked Sue.

"There at the cell house. It too is secured. We will never be able to get in there. The scouts are the only two that have access to the cell house—and, of course, the warden. To gain access, you need two keys, and a special key card. It takes three people to simultaneously gain entrance," Sue said.

Dax pulled out the devices that Fadez had given him.

"Will these gain us access?"

The two keys were oddly shaped, and the key card resembled a credit card; it was all black with a silver stripe down the middle.

"Yes, I believe these are the keys," Sue confirmed, handing the keys back to Dax.

"Who's going with me, and who's staying?" Blaze asked.

"I'll go. This time, we will return with all the girls," Seven said, looking at Kiaya.

Blaze, Dax, and Seven left for the cell house. Que and Breeze stayed at the shore with Sue and Kiaya.

"We are looking for a young lady, about your height, brown skin. She was last seen wearing a sweater. Her hair is in a twisted style."

"They're here," Ivy whispered to Staxx.

Four men entered the room with assault rifles. Night quickly pulled out his moon knives and attacked the men. He engaged in close combat with them, preventing them from using their weapons. He swung the crescent knives, cutting the guns in half and slicing the four guards' limbs off. The four guards moaned in agony.

"Let's move," Night said.

"Your friend that you are looking for—she's in the cell house with the other girls," Ivy said.

Zaina heard footsteps approaching the room, and she quickly placed her back against the wall next to the door. She slowly grasped her swords and instantly felt the power of the warrior queen of Ghana! She pulled the blades out of their holsters and stepped out of the room. Approaching the room were Blaze, Seven, and Dax. Zaina exhaled as she secured her weapons.

"It's ok. It's my brother, Dax, and Blaze."

Staxx, Night, and Ivy walked out of the room.

"You found her!" Blaze said with a relief.

Ivy looked confused about why they were looking for her.

"That's...not her," Seven slowly said.

"Who is she?" Dax asked.

"This is Ivy. It seems like the warden has been using her for an experimental drug. She was given a placebo drug for the virus that Kiaya was injected with," Staxx said.

Night looked at Blaze.

"You look like you've been to hell and back," Night sarcastically said.

"Egypt's in trouble!" Blaze exclaimed.

"What do you mean?" Zaina asked.

"I had an encounter with this…monstrous man. Mungo. He spoke of Egypt and Brix as if he came into contact with them. I had him right where I wanted him, then all of my powers drained," Blaze growled, hitting the wall.

"Wait. Did you say you had an encounter with Mungo?" Dax asked.

"Yes. Mungo—he came out of some sort of portal, a dark hole. The warden had pictures of..."

Blaze stopped and looked at Ivy. Everyone looked at Blaze, waiting for him to finish.

"There was a brief case with tubes of blood and pictures of girls. That's when I saw Egypt's picture," Blaze explained.

"We were headed to the cell house, but we decided to stop here first. Can you make it to the shore?"

Ivy nodded her head.

"Our people will be there to lead you off of the island, and we will rescue the other girls," Dax said.

"We can't just send her by herself. She's been through enough already," Staxx said.

"Then you go with her," Blaze said as he walked out of the room.

"Blaze! Wait!" Seven yelled as Blaze left.

"We're not splitting up anymore; we all have to stay together. There is an evil force out there that is hunting us for prey," Seven said.

"Yes, and his name is Mungo. I'm going to hunt him before he gets another chance to hunt us!" Blaze yelled down the hall of the hospital.

"I'll be fine. I know a short cut out of here that will lead me to the shore," Ivy said.

Zaina opened her frock and pulled out one of her swords.

"Use this to defend yourself." Zaina said as she handed Ivy the large dagger.

"Follow the ocean that is ascending in the sky. It will guide you to our people," Seven said to Ivy.

The Beings left the room, and Ivy went in the opposite direction.

"Yo!" Dax yelled at Blaze. "He's going after Mungo." Dax whispered.

The Beings all made it outside of the hospital. The sun was slowly rising. The view of the sunrise and the ocean in the sky was breathtaking. The ocean aligned with the sun created a subtle orange, still blue, and serene red that was tranquil. The golden rays shined through the ocean, illuminating the sea animals. They arrived at the cell house; it was secured with flesh-tearing barbwire. Several pit bulls circled the inside of the fence, sniffing the ground, moving at a rapid pace. No one wanted to approach the dogs; they all stood outside of the fence, plotting the best way to enter. Night took out his moon knives and slashed through the fence. He pulled the fence apart and stepped through. He looked at Staxx, and the pit bulls came running toward him. They continued to trot, saliva dangling from their mouths as their instincts compelled them to lock their jaws and shake the limbs of flesh.

"Staxx!" Night yelled as one of the pit bulls jumped toward his arm.

Staxx quickly touched his temple, and the pit bull fell out of the air. The other dogs stopped in their tracks. They started panting, their tongues leaning out the sides of their mouths. Dax crouched down and began to pet them. He reached into his backpack and pulled out some snacks, and he fed the dogs and instantly bonded with them. Staxx removed his finger from his temple and the dogs were released.

"It's ok, they've been mistreating you. I know," Dax said to the dogs as he continued to feed and pet them.

The Beings quickly walked past the dogs and made for the front of the cell house. Dax grabbed a handful of the snacks and tossed it out of the fence. The dogs quickly ran after the food. He gestured his hands in a rising motion, and two small trees barricaded the hole. Dax looked at the four dogs and smiled; he turned around and quickly caught back up with the others.

"What did you give them?"

"Just something I whipped up."

"Do you have the keys?"

Dax patted his pockets in search for the three keys. He pulled out the two oddly shaped keys and the key card. He handed one of the keys to Seven and the other to Zaina. Night and Staxx pulled out their weapons.

"On the count of three. One…two…three!"

Ivy made it out of the hospital. She looked up and couldn't deny the ocean shooting up into the sky; the Beings spoke of this.

"Follow the ocean," she said as she gripped the sword. She stumbled to the back entrance of the warden's mansion. She looked at the sword, and her confidence grew as she felt the spirit of Yaa Ashantewaa. She looked at the hospital band on her wrist and yanked it with force, but it wouldn't tear. The door was unlocked, so she slowly entered. Ivy wanted to unleash vengeance on the warden for all the physical pain and mental suffering he'd inflicted on her. She headed to his bedroom up the stairs. She approached his large room and had flashbacks of the room. Her head began to pound as she lost focus. She dropped the sword and held her head in an attempt to sooth the splitting migraine that traveled between her eyes, back and forth to her head. The clanging sound of the sword hitting the marble floor alerted someone in the closet. She felt someone approaching her. Her head was in so much pain that it hurt her to open her eyes. She grabbed the sword and pointed it upward at whomever was approaching her.

"Hand carved from the soul tree itself, forged by the village elders from the Ashanti Tribe."

Ivy's headache slowly went away, and she opened her eyes and looked up, still pointing the large dagger.

"Where…is…the warden?"

"I'm afraid that he has left the building."

Ivy stood up; her vision was impaired from the headache. She saw a blurred image of a large man that stood in front of the blade, holding a large duffle bag. His abdominal and neck were wrapped in bandage. She started sobbing, a mixture of emotions running through her mind.

"Where is the warden?" She asked, sniffing and sobbing.

"Your tears lead me the believe that he has done something terrible to you."

"Don't move. I'm not even supposed to be in here. I am supposed to follow the water in the sky! I don't know. I am to meet some special people that will take me away from this dreadful place."

"I can help you. Come with me, and I will guarantee you the vengeance that you seek."

Ivy slowly lowered the blade. She wiped her eyes and was comforted by Mungo. She continued to cry while Mungo gracefully took the sword out of her hand. He gently placed it in his duffle bag.

"What is your name?"

"Ivy."

"I will take care of you," Mungo said, placing his arm around her and walking her out of the room. The warden watched as they walked down the stairs. He inconspicuously followed them as they walk to the active portal.

"Hey!" Blaze yelled as he saw Mungo walking through the portal, with his arm around Ivy.

Ivy quickly looked back. Mungo pulled her by her wrist, diverting her from the distraction. The hospital wristband slipped from Ivy's wrist and fell outside of the portal.

Blaze ran to the portal after Mungo. He sent a furry of lightning bolts into the portal as it began to close. The lightning latched onto the portal! Blaze then began to stretch the hole open.

"Ahhhhh!" he yelled as the hole opened just enough for him to jump in!

"Where are you?" Blaze yelled into the dark hole. He hit his fists together to ignite an electrical charge. Blaze walked through the portal; he noticed the flickering sound of electricity amplifying as he approached the end of the portal. He stepped out of the portal and bumped into Myles and Fadez.

The heavy door to the cell house clicked.

"Mask on!" Staxx said.

The Beings pulled their masks over their faces, only revealing their eyes. Night and Staxx walked in front as the door cracked open. Rows of guards stood ten feet away from the door. The guards were armed with see-through fiberglass shields, titanium helmets, combat boots, bulletproof vests, and AR-15s. The guards all pointed their guns at Night and Staxx. They were organized and moved as a unit. The scene was intimidating for those who were faint of heart.

"Remain calm." Staxx's thoughts transferred to the Beings.

Night looked around the cell house; there were guards by each cell, guarding the girls. There were two girls in each cell. One girl walked to the iron bars that were located on the second level, and her eyes were filled with hope and courage.

"No justice, no peace!" she yelled from the cell.

The guard quickly turned around and hit her in the head with the butt of the gun. The girl's body fell down, and she looked up at the ceiling, blood flowing down from her forehead and into her eyes. She gazed at an American flag poster plastered on the ceiling. The blood in her eyes change her perspective of the American flag. Now it seemed to run with blood. Zaina leaped in the air, and she pulled out her dagger. She stood face to face with the two guards. She quickly attacked the guards and tossed them over the ledge. The guard's bodies dropped in front of the other guards.

All the girls in the cells cheered her on and banged the iron bars on the cells. The Beings had declared war!

Zaina stuck her hand through the iron bar and wiped the blood off of the young black girl's face. The girl's eyes opened as Zaina used her healing hands.

"Stay down. Thank you for your courage," Zaina said to the young girl.

The Beings began to engage in battle with the armed guards. Their powers were on full display. Night took off his shades and blinded the guards with the bright light that came from his eyes. He then began to engage in close combat with his crescent moon knives. Dax pulled out his bow and arrows and shot the arrows at the guards, piercing through their vests. Staxx looked for the control room that was located in the corner. He made his way to the room, and he slowly pulled out his sword, which was in a holster on his back. Three guards stood in front of the door. Bullets came soaring at Staxx from the guard's guns. Staxx released the sword, and it began to move, blocking all the bullets to protect him. He walked toward the guards as they reloaded their guns and continued to shoot at him. He pulled the small dagger that was attached to his right Achilles' heel, and he disarmed the guards with the small dagger, and they all got on their knees. Using his telekinetic powers, he removed the plastic handcuffs from their belts and cuffed them.

"You'll never make it out of here alive," one of the guards said.

The sword that had blocked the bullets continued to levitate. The sword slowly entered back into the holster on Staxx's back. The three watched as Staxx walked over to the guard. He looked down and saw the keys to the control room. He yanked the keys off of the guard's belt. He then cut the plastic cuff, releasing the guard. He lifted his joggers and placed the small dagger back into the brace that protected his Achilles' heel.

"What were you saying again?"

The guard slowly stood up and pulled knives from the sides of his pants. He charged at Staxx, swinging the knives wildly. Staxx dodged every attempt. Staxx backed up and planted his right foot. The guard lunged the knives toward Staxx's heart, but Staxx remained calm. He completed a round-house kick with his right leg, connecting with the side of the guard's face. Crack! The guard's neck snapped from the power of his right leg. The guard fell to the floor. No signs of life remained in his body. One of the guards focused on the brace as Staxx rolled down his joggers. Staxx unlocked the door and entered the control room.

Seven's eyes began to glow with a bright orange hue, along with his fist! He then levitated off of the ground. He lifted his hands up, and the guards lifted up! He brought all the guards into the center. He forcefully moved his hands down! All the guards came crashing down onto the floor, their bones shattering on top of one another. Seven descended to the ground as the Beings watched. The Beings all heard the unlocking and clanking of the cell doors opening. The girls all hurried out of the cells. The Beings tried to pick Lauryn out of the crowd, but there were too many girls.

Staxx searched the room until he came across an inmate attendance sheet. He looked at the list of names listed in the book. He moved his finger up and down on the list, reading each name.

"Do you see her?" Staxx yelled as he ran out of the control room, holding the book of names.

"Lauryn! Lauryn!" Night yelled, his voice echoing through the cell house.

"We have to go! We have to meet back up with Breeze and Que," Zaina said.

"Everyone listen up! We are all going to get out of here together. Alive. We are going to form three lines and head to the shore."

Night looked around the room at the girls and ladies. They were distressed. Some of them held hands, and most of them stood against the walls.

"We are not here to hurt you. We are here to help; we are looking for a friend. Lauryn is her name," Night said.

The crowd slowly dispersed as an inmate approached. She held one hand over her belly and her other on her lower back. Liquid oozed down her leg as she panted. She started rapidly breathing with short breaths. She fell to her knees.

"Mmmm...ahhh," she screamed in agony.

"There's a baby in that belly," Dax said.

Zaina walked over to the lady to comfort her. She took off her gloves and smiled.

"What's your name?" Zaina asked, softly rubbing her forehead.

She began to rapidly breathe again; she grabbed Zaina's hand and squeezed it. She screamed again.

"Relax. Your contractions are close. Your baby is coming," Zaina said.

"My name is Tuesday. I don't want to have my baby in this...jail."

Seven knelt down with Zaina and Tuesday.

"Can I be an assistance for you?" Seven asked.

"Yes, grab some blankets and towels. We are headed outside."

Seven stood up and walked to one of the cells, which was open. He pulled the blanket off of the bed, along with the sheets. Staxx and Night helped carry Tuesday out of the jail, and the group of girls followed.

"Wait. My baby's father—he's still inside."

"A guard?" Dax asked.

Staxx began to gaze into Tuesday's eyes. He quickly traveled through her memory and found her baby's father.

"He's in the hole," Staxx said.

"Yes, how do you know…wuh…wuh…This baby is moving around!" She said as she felt another contraction.

"I'll find him," Dax said.

"Wait, I'll come with you."

All the inmates hurried outside. Seven and Staxx laid the sheets and blanket on the lawn and assisted Tuesday onto the ground. Zaina closed her eyes and began to gently glide her soft hands over Tuesday's belly. Zaina's hands began to glow, which made Tuesday's belly transparent. Tuesday looked down and saw her belly glowing.

"Is that my baby inside?" she asked with a mix of emotions. She felt joyful to see a being that grew inside of her for nine months. She also was petrified that she would have to push her baby out of her.

"Yes," Zaina said with a warm smile. "Relax…Relax…Relax. Your baby is ready to enter the world. Are you ready to push?"

"Woo…woo…woo! Yes!"

Tuesday tried to turn around, but she was quickly drawn back from a sharp pain.

Several minutes passed as Zaina coached Tuesday through her labor.

"I need you to give me one final push. Remember, push from your stomach and don't yell. Let your body vibrate the energy from within."

Dax, Night, and a man ran out of the cell house to Tuesday. Zaina nodded her head, and Tuesday pushed!

The man ran to Tuesday and grabbed her hand.

"I'm here with you, baby!" he said, kissing her forehead.

"One more push," Zaina said.

Tuesday mustered her last bit of energy and pushed with all of her strength. Having her partner by her side motivated her. She looked ahead and saw a mountain-sized stream of water soaring in the sky. A small cry appeared from below. Tuesday opened her arms and received the life that had grown inside of her. Zaina handed her a towel, and she gently cleaned her baby boy.

"What shall we name him?"

Tuesday looked at the ocean that ascended into the sky. The path was set. She looked around at all the girls who had been tricked into the system. She started to weep.

"Moses. You are going to be a great leader. Just like Moses of Egypt, you will lead your people and guide them, just as these angels have done for us."

Dax created a bed out of the tree branches, leaves, and dirt. They assisted Tuesday on the bed so she could lie down and nurse her baby.

"What about Lauryn?" Night asked.

"She is alive. I can feel it. We have to trust the journey," Staxx answered.

"Let's head back," Zaina suggested.

Zaina and the Beings packed up and headed back to the shore. Then all the inmates followed them as they left the cell house.

Chapter 15:

REDEMPTION

"I'll be right back!" Breeze said to Que, Kiaya, and Sue.

He walked down to the ocean, where he'd had the encounter with the large shark. The shark was dead, lifeless. He pushed the shark back into the water. He closed his eyes and followed the shark. Breeze began to float in place, and the shark's eyes opened. Breeze showed no fear as he stood in front of the large shark; he floated closer. He moved to the shark's gills and began to subtly whisper to it. The shark moved back a few feet and quickly swung its tail at Breeze. Breeze went soaring upward in the water! The shark then took off after Breeze, hunting his prey.

Breeze looked up and saw the clouds; he then completed a back-flip and landed on the shark's back. He grabbed the shark by its large dorsal fin. The shark moved its body in an attempt to throw Breeze off. Breeze held on to gain control of the shark. They tussled in the water for several minutes until the shark gave in. Breeze slowly removed himself from the shark's back. The shark rapidly turned to face Breeze, gazing at him with his small black eyes! Breeze stuck out his hand toward the shark's mouth and rubbed it on its large snout. The shark lowered its snout for several seconds while Breeze floated in place. Breeze looked to the left and saw a blurry vision of what seemed like a herd approaching the shore. He hopped on the shark's back, and they fled to the bottom of the ocean. Breeze hopped off the shark and landed back on the land. The shark then glided through the water.

Breeze ran down the path to what seemed like a mirage when he reached the land. He looked around. He couldn't believe what he saw. He saw his family, along with several girls wearing jail attire. Hundreds and thousands of girls all together. He walked over to Night and the others.

"Did you find her?"

Night slowly exhaled, lowering his head. Breeze looked at Tuesday, who was being carried by a man and Night.

"Where's Blaze, Myles, and Fadez?"

Que and Dax looked at each other.

"The portal!" they said in unison.

"Myles and Fadez went after Mungo, who they believe came out of a portal. We need to head back to the warden's house," Que said.

"Has a young girl approached you? I believe her name is Ivy," Zaina asked Que.

"No, she hasn't."

"So, what do we do now?" Zaina asked.

Seven walked over to Breeze, and he looked at the ocean.

"How long can you keep the path clear?" he asked.

"As long as my black diamond is buried in the sand, the path will remain clear. As soon as it is pulled from the earth, the ocean will fall back in place."

"We have to get them to the other side safely," Breeze said.

"That's about a twenty-five-mile walk on feet," Seven said.

Seven went over to Monk, who was with his family.

"How's he doing?" Seven asked Monk, peeking at the baby.

"He's sleeping now."

"Are you ok?" Seven asked Tuesday.

"Yes. I'm just tired."

"I need you to lead your family and the girls off of this Island."

"What do you mean?"

"Follow me."

Seven, along with the Beings and Monk, walked to the beginning of the path, where the water separated.

"This path will lead you off of the island onto the land. Help will be waiting for you on the other side to provide aid and care."

"What about protection from the guards? When I realized what type of evil work was being practiced on this island, it was too late. They tossed me into the hole. I am ashamed of being a guard on this island. I'm sure there are more waiting for a vulnerable moment," Monk said.

"I have a few friends who will protect you along your journey," Breeze added.

Breeze looked at the water and then at the girls.

"I have an idea!" he exclaimed.

Breeze ran down the path, where he'd planted the black diamond.

"Everyone get back on the land!" he yelled from a distance.

"Get back on the land," Staxx informed everyone.

They all eased back from the clear path onto the grassland. Breeze stuck his hand into the earth and moved it around until he felt the diamond. He closed his eyes and pulled the diamond out of the sand. The ocean made a loud roar as it descended from the sky. Animals fell from the sky to be placed back into the water. The water forcefully hit the bottom and scaled back up. The ocean settled as the animals swam freely. The water was still. Breeze remained at the bottom of the ocean, clutching his black diamond in his palm. He placed the diamond back on his necklace to secure it as he walked under the water. As he continued to walk, the ocean started to ripple. The large shark approached Breeze and floated in front of him. Breeze placed his head on the shark's snout and gently rubbed his head. The shark then performed a 180-degree circle and took off. Breeze swam to the shore and walked back on the land.

A large dorsal fin appeared out of the water, and the girls became frightened. The shark jumped out of the water and dove back under.

"It's ok," Breeze confirmed.

The shark then appeared in the shallow water.

"Shadow will be your guide; he will make sure that everyone makes it to the other side safely," Breeze said.

"How is he going to transport everyone?" Dax asked.

A wave emerged from the ocean, and a multitude of sharks arrived in the shallow water. Moments later, an army of dolphins appeared, jumping in and out of the water. Countless sharks and dolphins had arrived.

"Your Uber has arrived," Breeze said jokingly.

Breeze and Seven walked over to Monk, and his family and assisted them onto Shadow. Once everyone saw that the sharks were calm and there to help, they too became confident and walked toward the water. A girl stepped into the shallow water, and a dolphin swam to her and rubbed its snout against her ankle. The dolphin moved its tail up and down and began to echo and whistle.

"It's ok. She wants you to get on her," Breeze said to the girl.

The girl got on the dolphin, and they swam out farther into the ocean. The other girls followed and mounted the rest of the dolphins and sharks. Seven walked over to Kiaya to help her get onto a shark.

"What do you plan to do now?"

"First, I'm going home and taking me a hot shower. Then I will go to MTR HAIRapy for some needed attention. After that, I will organize a protest to bring awareness to this issue," Kiaya said as she looked at all the girls who'd been taken from their families.

"Will I ever see you again?" Kiaya asked.

"Yes. I am sure that we will meet up again."

"Thank you, Seven," she said, offering Seven her hand.

Seven leaned in and hugged her.

"Thank you. Be safe, Kiaya."

All the girls were secured on the sharks and dolphins. Shadow led the pack with Monk and his family on his back. The Beings stood at the edge of the water until all the girls were out of their sight.

"Well done, Breeze…Well done."

Seven, Breeze, Zaina, Que, Night, Dax, and Staxx stood by the water, lost for words. Staxx began to softly sing.

"Old pirates, yes they robbed I, Sold I to the merchant ships, minutes after they took I, from the bottomless pit, but my hand was made strong. By the hand of the almighty, we forward in this generation, triumphantly."

The Beings looked at Staxx and joined in.

They all started singing "Redemption Song" by Bob Marley while the sun set over the ocean.

Chapter 16:

GATECRASHING

"How did you like the tour of my island?" Queen Dahlia asked.

Soulek smiled as he received the praise from the Queen for seizing Lauryn. Queen Dahlia saw the smile on Soulek's face from her peripheral. At this moment, Lauryn decided to engage in conversation with Queen Dahlia to display her confidence. She chose her words carefully; too much dialogue with the Queen could be dangerous.

"I didn't get much of a tour. Your hospitality skills could use some polishing. By the way, I haven't eaten since I was brought here against my will," Lauryn said.

Queen Dahlia chuckled. "Generosity is a weakness that I am personally working on."

The Queen looked to her left and gestured for one of the soul seekers to leave the room. She walked over to where Soulek had securely placed Lauryn. She lifted the heavy gauntlets with her hands and examined them thoroughly.

"I see that Lord Salvo responded promptly. He never disappoints me; his constant delivery is a skill that could be learned," Queen Dahlia said as she admired the gauntlets that covered Lauryn's hands.

Soulek felt unappreciated. He knew that he had accomplished a task that none of Dahlia's soldiers could have done.

"The details are fascinating! Each slot for your finger is secured with the most durable metal from the Dark Realm. Consider them a gift."

Dahlia let go of the heavy gauntlet, and they fell into Lauryn's lap.

"What's the Dark Realm?" Lauryn asked.

"Close your eyes. Souls wander the land helplessly, looking for aid. Light does not exist. Your vibrant energy is snatched as soon as you enter. The life is sucked out of you and formatted into negative energy. Yes, the Dark Realm can be the strongest reality on earth. Lord Salvo's fire is the only beacon in this realm," Dahlia explained.

A thunderous knock at the door resounded throughout the room. Soulek quickly went to the large wooden doors and opened them. Mungo stood in the doorway, a large duffle bag in one hand.

"You're late," Soulek whispered.

Soulek looked at Ivy, confused. He then stepped to the side to allow them both to enter. Mungo walked in, carrying his bag of weapons that he'd obtained on his journey. He walked and stood in front of Queen Dahlia, dropping the bag.

"I come bearing gifts," Mungo said as he knelt.

The Queen looked down at Mungo's back, which displayed his war wounds.

"You didn't inform me that you were bringing a guest."

Mungo stood up and introduced Ivy.

"This is Ivy. She was caught wandering. I suppose she can be of good use to your movement."

"I don't need a little girl for what I'm doing! Your obsessive compulsiveness for weapons is the reason you are always unpunctual. You were sent to retrieve two items! In return, you brought back a girl and a bag of junk that I have no use for."

The Queen was furious with Mungo; her patience was thin, as there was no room for failure.

Mungo looked at Ivy and nodded his head. Ivy reached behind her and pulled out a Golden Dagger.

"Please accept this gift as a token for my gatecrashing," Ivy said.

The Queen gazed at the Golden Dagger that gracefully lay in Ivy's palms. Gently, she picked it up. Lauryn looked at Ivy as she trembled with fear. Mungo rubbed Ivy's back with his enormous hand, calming her down with every stroke. The Queen assessed the Golden Dagger; she removed the glove from her left hand and pricked the top of her index finger. Two drops of blood oozed out.

"The blade is sharp. Where's the other? You were supposed to bring back two Golden Daggers."

Dahlia placed the Golden Dagger into an empty holster. She now held two of the Golden Daggers in her possession. Mungo explained that he would need more time to find the other dagger. Mungo and Queen Dahlia began to speak over each other as Ivy discreetly looked at Lauryn. Ivy lowered her head quickly when she and Lauryn made eye contact. Ivy looked at Lauryn again, this time noticing her flawless brown skin and twisted hair. Her eyes stretched wide open as she gasped!

Dax and Que led the others through the large mansion back to the area where they'd found Blaze. The portal flickered and crackled with electricity.

"Myles and Fadez went in here. They went after Mungo," Dax said.

"Where does this dark hole lead to?"

Staxx looked down, and he noticed a hospital wristband. He picked up the wristband and looked at the numbers; he then placed his index and middle fingers onto his temple and closed his eyes.

Ivy screamed out, "It's you! You are Lauryn!"

Everyone looked at Ivy. Queen Dahlia yanked Ivy by her gown.

"What do you know about her?" The Queen asked.

"Who said that? Stop that! Get out of my head!" Ivy screamed.

Meanwhile, Lauryn watched as Ivy screamed and yelled.

"Ivy…It's Staxx. Where are you?" Staxx's voiced echoed in her head.

"I see her! I'm looking right at her!" Ivy exclaimed as she pointed at Lauryn.

"Who are you talking to?" The Queen asked.

The Beings flocked around Staxx.

Soulek stuck his hand out, and a soul seeker placed a syringe in it. He walked up to Ivy and jabbed the needle into her neck.

"Ivy! Ivy! She's gone," Staxx said.

Ivy lost conscious, and Mungo caught her right before she hit the ground, with the syringe bulging out of the side of her neck. Mungo glared at Soulek, simmering with rage.

"Stay focused. Now is not the time for a clash. We have a guest. Control yourself. She was a liability, and you brought her unannounced," The Queen said.

"This isn't over. You'll pay for this," Mungo whispered to Soulek as he laid Ivy down on the ground, slowly removing the syringe from her neck.

The Beings looked at Staxx to say something.

"She said she saw Lauryn and she was looking right at her. She must have dropped her band before entering in here," Staxx said, showing the wristband.

He looked at the wristband and tucked it into his pocket.

"There. That should fix it," Breeze said.

Breeze tapped the wristband on his wrist and then tapped the device behind his ear.

"Yo, yo, yo," Breeze said.

"Breeze?" Myles asked.

"Yeah, it's me. Where are you guys?" Breeze asked.

Myles, Fadez, and Blaze looked at a large wooden sign decorated with rusted nails.

"Ile Du Diable," Myles said.

"What did he say?" Dax asked.

"Devil's Island," Seven answered.

Blaze heard the electricity crackling from the portal through the device.

"This is Blaze talking. Where are you guys?"

"We're in the mansion, right next to the portal," Dax said.

"You all are going to have to take turns walking through the portal. Zaina! You are first," Blaze said.

Zaina gathered her belongings and looked at the Beings.

"See you on the other side," she said as she walked through the portal.

"Zaina. Zaina!" Seven said through his communication device.

"I made it through! I'm with Myles, Blaze, and Fadez," Zaina said.

"Staxx, you're next," Blaze said.

Staxx slowly walked through the portal and saw Zaina's hand on the other side. He grabbed her hand and was pulled out of the portal.

"I'm good!" Staxx confirmed.

"Let's go, Dax," Blaze said.

"Nah, Night, you go ahead," Dax said.

Night took off his shades and illuminated the portal. The Beings on the other side saw a bright light coming as he approached. They pulled Night out of the portal, and he placed his shades back on to cover his eyes.

Seven stepped into the portal and was pulled out by Night. A blue flame emerged, and Night pulled Que out of the portal.

"Ok, Dax, it's on you. Let's go!

"Dax! The portal is closing! We need you to come through now!" Blaze shouted.

Blaze ran to the portal and tried to expand it. The portal's magnetic force field was too powerful. Que and Myles gave Blaze a hand. It was too late. The portal diminished and vanished.

"Dax…Dax…Dax…Dax…Daaaaax!"

Chapter 17:

UPRISING

Mungo picked Ivy up in his arms and walked to the exit.

"Where are you going? We are not quite finish here."

Four soul seekers stood in front of the exit, blocking Mungo from leaving. Mungo smirked and turned around.

"Come eat...Relax yourself...You have been through a lot, and it has not gone unnoticed. Place the girl next to the souvenir," Queen Dahlia said.

Two soul seekers took Ivy from Mungo's arms and placed her behind the large throne, where Lauryn was tied up.

"What have they done to her?" Lauryn asked.

The soul seeker glanced at Lauryn and quickly gagged her mouth to prevent her from talking.

Mungo gaped at Queen Dahlia, as her beauty drew him in. Soulek was disgusted with the Queen for ignoring his achievement but bringing light to his failures. He left the room and slammed the door behind him, causing a painting to fall off of the wall. Mungo attempted to go after Soulek, but Dahlia placed her hand on his chest. He looked down at her hand.

"We have work to do. You need to rest and regain your energy and strength. I can get used to having you around. A king of your magnitude is needed for the throne."

"What about your yes man?"

"Soulek is weak. His will to lead is overshadowed with black clouds of doubt. To be a leader, you have to be fierce! You have to do what is right for your followers, even if lives are sacrificed in the process," Dahlia said as she turned and looked at Lauryn.

"Come here, boys…Come here, boys."

The four pit bulls came running toward Dax, and they jumped up on him, bringing him to the ground. They began to lick his face and tussle with him. Dax rolled around with the dogs and laughed. One of the dogs stopped rolling around and lifted his head up. The dog took off running up the stairs, and the others followed. Dax jumped up and went after the dogs, racing up the staircase. The sound of screaming and growling echoed inside the room. Dax swiftly entered the room and saw a man standing on top of a dresser, protecting himself with a briefcase.

"Mr. Bennett?"

The dogs ran over to Dax once they'd heard his voice. Dax looked at Mr. Bennett as he slowly petted the dogs to calm them down. Once the dogs were calm, Mr. Bennett climbed down from the dresser and brushed his clothes off. Dax stared at him with several questions to ask.

"This day has been nothing short of interesting," Mr. Bennett said, picking up his briefcase.

"You seem familiar. Have we met before?"

"What's in the briefcase?"

"I've already been through this today," he said while slowly reaching in his waistband.

One of the dogs started growling as the warden pointed a gun at Dax. Dax looked at the gun with the syringe filled with gray liquid.

"Now, I'm going to walk out of here unbothered. You and those mutts are going to go your separate ways, and no one will get hurt."

"So, you were the one that enslaved all of the girls. Why?"

"You know you people ask too many questions!"

"You people?" Dax chuckled. "My people are chosen by God. What makes you think that you can just enslave a group of people, hold them against their will, and oppress them? I never did like your history class; American history was built on the backs of my ancestors. We built this country for free. All American history books in the school system should be burned! White supremacy will be dismantled. Every Confederate statue will be brought down and crumbled to ashes!" Dax ranted.

The warden slowly backed up to a window.

"You fool! You have no authority here! It's too late. The seed has been planted in America's soil! We've won! You kill each other and bring each other down as soon as we let one of your kind make it to the top. Your race is self-destructive. Yes! We did rob you of your culture and made you pray to a blond-haired blue-eyed God! Your people did build this country on free labor! Fools." The warden laughed.

"My people will rise! Our God has provided us with the power and gifts to bring down cowards such as yourself! My generation is the great, great grandchildren of slaves that fought and escaped! You cannot keep your feet on our necks. Your hatred of history is being erased! No one will remember what was. God's children will rise to the great nation that he built us to be! Love will flourish throughout the land, and hate will be forgotten!"

The warden squeezed the trigger. Dax quickly grabbed his hand and punched him in his face. The warden stumbled back to the window, causing the glass to crack. Dax kicked him in the chest, causing the window to shatter as the warden's back went through it.

Dax walked to the window and quickly pulled out his bow, along with two black arrows. He placed the arrows on the bowstring and pulled the string back. He squinted as he watched the warden falling. Dax released the bow string, and the two arrows went flying past the warden. The warden smirked at Dax as the arrows missed him. Dax gently blew air from his mouth, glaring down at the warden. The two arrows separated and plunged into the water. The arrows then completed a U-turn and shot out of the water, piercing through the warden's left and right hand. A big ripple formed in the water from the impact of the body. The ocean slowly turned red as the warden vanished.

Dax walked over to the briefcase that was locked. He bent down to his ankle and pulled out his knife. He picked the briefcase lock with the knife and placed it back into its holster on his ankle. Several pictures of girls were scattered in the briefcase. Dax found a five-by-seven picture and the numbers 43520003. The back of the picture read, "Successful match. Same blood type and successful replica of DNA strands to compliment Egypt. 'Prototype.'"

"This can't be," Dax said as he stared at the picture.

"Can anybody hear me? Come in! Can anybody hear me?" Dax asked.

"Yes. We can hear you. What happened? Why didn't you come through the portal?"

"I went back for the dogs. I couldn't just leave them stranded like that. Never mind that. I ran into the warden and came across a briefcase with several pictures of the girls that were rescued. I came across a large picture with the numbers 43520003 and a young girl. On the back of the picture, it reads, 'Successful match. Same blood type and successful replica of DNA strands to compliment Egypt. Prototype."

Staxx reached into his pocket and pulled out Ivy's hospital band.
"43520003," he read.
The Beings all looked at one another, confused.

Chapter 18:

PREPARATION MEETS OPPORTUNITY

Dax closed the briefcase and went on a tour through the large mansion. The four dogs followed him as he walked, in search of more clues.

"Dax, can you hear me?"

"Yes. I'm here."

"Listen. We need you to get out of there. That island is not safe, and you're alone," Staxx said.

Dax walked up to a locked door and picked it with his knife. He opened the door and saw several flat-screen monitors plastered on the walls.

"I'm going to be here for a while. I found the security room," Dax said.

"Be safe," Staxx said.

Dax walked over to a large bin and opened it. Inside were old cassette tapes dated back to the 1980's. He sat in a chair and viewed the large control panel that was lit up. All the buttons were overwhelming.

"I could really use Breeze's brains right now," Dax said to himself.

He began to type and push buttons, which disabled the control monitor. The control monitor locked and shut down. Dax felt defeated as he began to hit the panel. He sighed and laid his head on the keyboard. He turned to his left and saw a calendar with the date highlighted. He viewed the calendar, which read, "Planter arriving today." Dax stood up and looked out of the window. A large ship was approaching the island.

"This is the captain. I repeat, this is the captain."

Dax hurried to the communication device, pressed the button on the side, and spoke.

"I'm here," he said, trying to disguise his voice.

"We're about five miles away from the drop-off. There were no guards on duty. Is everything ok?"

"Yes, everything is ok. Just come to the drop-off spot and proceed as usual," Dax said.

"Ten-four."

Dax squinted and looked out of the window. He saw insides the ship that was miles away. He saw armed guards and girls shackled inside of the ship.

"This can't be," Dax said.

He quickly grabbed his things and headed to the warden's room. There, he found a large pea coat, scarf, and fedora that disguised him. He took off his bow and arrow and held it close to his side, where the large coat covered it. The sun had set, and it was dark outside. The loud ship horn echoed throughout the island upon the ship's arrival. Dax watched as it pulled up to the side of the large hospital. The bright light shined on Dax as he gestured his hand to show that the light was too bright. The large anchors were lowered, and three guards lowered a bridge to walk from the ship to the island. Dax walked to the bridge and greeted the guards.

"Welcome back. How was your trip? Dax said.

"Not bad at all, sir," One of the guards replied.

Dax kept his head angled away from the guards and stayed several feet away from them.

"Where would you like us to take the cargo?"

"The same as before," Dax answered.

Dax sized the guards up to see if they were strapped. They only had pistols. *I can take these guys*, he thought to himself.

The foghorn blasted. A short, round white man walked off of the ship, wearing a white coat and captain hat.

"This place seems empty; I would say I like what you've done with the place, but I would be lying," the short man said, approaching Dax.

"Well, I decided to give everyone the night off," Dax replied.

"Why would you do that?" the short man inquired.

"I'm kidding," Dax said, imitating the warden's chuckle.

The short man laughed as he patted Dax on the shoulder, walking past him.

"I can really use a double scotch on the rocks."

"Well, make yourself at home, you know where I keep all the good stuff. Dax said.

"Let me see what you brought me," Dax said as he walked to the ship.

One of the guards stopped him, placing his hand on Dax's chest.

"Come on, you know the rules."

"You're right," Dax said as he tried to think of a plan.

"The captain get first dibs, then you," the guard said.

"Come on. How about that drink?" The captain said from a distance.

Dax turned around and proceeded to walk back to the warden's mansion. The three guards stayed and guarded the ship entrance.

"You know, I have something I want you to try. I've been saving it for a special night," Dax said.

The captain walked through a side door to the mansion.

"I hand-selected your girl for tonight. I'm sure she will bring you much pleasure. She was picked up from one of those HBCU. You know, the black colleges."

"Oh really? Tell me more," Dax said, opening the door.

The captain went to explain, "Story has it, we sent a gunman on the campus in Greensboro, North Carolina."

"A and T?"

"Yes! That campus. Beautiful place for the blacks," the captain said, chuckling.

Dax grew furious as he recalled the gunman on the campus of A and T.

"The gunman let off a few rounds, and the blacks all scattered like roaches! It was the most hilarious thing I've ever seen, especially when you know the outcome. So, this young freshman runs for safety and is confronted by our pathfinder. He leads her to safety in our vehicle and to the planter!" he said, laughing.

Dax clenched his fist, ready to steal off on the captain, but he regained his composure and waited. The captain continued to walk through the mansion to a bar area. He took off his hat and coat and placed them on the bar stool. Dax walked behind the counter and reached for a bottle on the top shelve. He then grabbed a glass and proceeded to pour a double shot. The captain took the double shot to the head and slammed the glass on the granite counter top.

"Ahh! I needed that. Hit me again."

Dax poured another double shot and slowly removed that fedora from off his head, revealing his face. The captain took the shot and closed his eyes tight.

"Whooo!" he exclaimed as the aged scotch trickled down his throat.

"What the—" the captain said as he saw Dax's face.

He fell off the stool and stumbled towards the door, ripping it open. He snatched his coat and hat from the floor and fled.

Dax lifted his hand and placed his left thumb and index in his mouth. He whistled.

The captain looked back, but he kept running. Suddenly, four dogs came soaring in his direction, and he quickly turned around and ran back to the door. He made it back into the barroom and slammed the door shut. Breathing heavily, he fell to his knees. He took a handkerchief out of his coat pocket and wiped the sweat away from his face. Dax took off the warden's attire and slowly walked to the captain.

"Empty your pockets and take off that coat," Dax ordered him.

"I don't have any money on me, only credit cards. Here! Take them all!"

"Give me your coat and your hat."

Dax grabbed the coat and searched the insides of the pockets. He found a smart phone that was unlocked, a wallet, and a set of keys.

The dogs scratched the door and snarled. The captain looked back at the door, terrified.

"What do you want with me?"

Dax slowly put his arm in the white coat and ignored the question the captain had raised.

"So, what do you call your yacht? I'm pretty sure you have a name for it. I'm not going to hurt you," Dax said.

The captain appeared relieved.

The captain glanced at the keys that Dax held securely in his palm. Dax slowly placed the keys in his pocket and actively listened to the captain.

"The Planter," the captain answered.

"Excuse me?" Dax said.

"Her name is the Planter."

Dax chuckled and shook his head. *The audacity*, Dax thought as he yanked the captain from the floor.

"How many girls are on the ship?"

"I don't know!" The captain whimpered.

Dax pulled his knife from its holster and placed the sharp blade against the captain's neck.

"How many girls are on the ship, and how many guards are there, all together?"

The blade began to prick the captain's flesh, and small droplets of blood leaked onto his collar.

"Fifteen girls and five guards! Three guards outside of the ship and two inside!"

Dax removed his knife from the captain's neck and gracefully placed it back into the holster.

"There. That wasn't so bad, was it?"

"What did you do to Bennett?"

Dax walked to the door, ignoring the captain. He flipped the light switch, and the room turned dark. Dax opened the door, and the four dogs rushed in. The door shut, and Dax walked off, gently placing the captain's hat on his head. The dogs indistinctly growled as the captain screamed in agony.

Dax viewed the guards, who were standing outside of the yacht, talking. The three guards laughed and flaunted their guns irresponsibly. He sighed and sat down and began to remove the captain's coat and hat.

"This is going to be a long night," Dax said to himself.

About an hour had passed, and Dax was still watching the guards from a distance. He noticed their body language changing as they grew restless. Their hands were off the triggers, and they had let up. He was very confident in his ability to send three arrows simultaneously that would take out the guards. He didn't want to alarm the other guards or place the girls in more danger, so he waited until preparation met opportunity. The three guards guarding the ship walked away from the dock, and Dax seized the moment.

He quickly put on the coat and placed the three arrows back into the holster on his back. He headed toward the dock but was suddenly alarmed by two guards walking across the bridge from the yacht. Dax quickly looked around to see if there was somewhere he could take shelter. There was nowhere to go! He knelt down on one knee and placed his right hand in the dirt. He looked down at his hand and noticed it camouflaging with the land that surrounded him. He pulled his hand up and looked at it; it was normal. He placed both hands back into the dirt, and they both started camouflaging. He took the coat off and threw it over his back and tucked his legs and arms in until they touched his chest. The sound of steps and rustling leaves approached.

"Yeah, that was him. Look, he left his hat," the guard said as he chuckled.

"He must have had too much to drink and was taking a little break on this tree stump. Let's head to the hospital to make sure they are ready for us to start unloading the girls."

The guards took the hat and walked toward the hospital. The large tree stump dissolved and turned into Dax. He removed the coat and stood up; he brushed the leaves and dirt off of himself and headed to the yacht. He arrived at the dock and walked across the bridge leading to the yacht. Once he'd crossed the bridge, he pressed a button that reeled it in. Dax found three large anchors that were submerged in the water. He pulled each anchor out of the water and headed inside of the large ship. He dropped everything in his hands and looked around. He counted exactly fifteen girls, who looked like they were around the ages of fourteen to twenty-three. Their mouths were muffled. Their wrists were bound to the bars with plastic handcuffs. Each one of them looked to be under the influence of a controlled substance, as they nodded in and out. He walked over to a young girl, who was within arm's reach of him, and gently lifted her head up. She spoke incoherently as drool glimmered from the side of her mouth. Dax gently lowered her head and reached for his knife. He pulled out the knife and cut the restraints from her wrists. The girl was exhausted as she lay on the floor of the yacht. Dax proceed to cut the restraints from the other girls. He came to the last girl; she looked older than the others, and she was wearing a black Civil Rights Museum t-shirt, with the collar cut out and the Greensboro Four on the front. She wore her hair in large corn rolls with gold clips through each braid. She wore black jeans with holes on each leg. She looked at Dax and watched his every move.

"Don't hurt them. They've been through enough already," she whispered to Dax.

"Trust me. I'm not here to hurt you."

"What are you doing then?"

"We are getting off of this island."

The young lady looked around and noticed that all the girls were released from the bars. Dax noticed that she was the only one not doped up.

"Can you take care of the others while I get this boat moving?" Dax asked.

The young lady looked at Dax, and then she glanced at all the girls. Some were lying down, and some of them were sitting up.

"Yeah, sure."

"Ok, great! Get them all some water and find some food. Keep them calm and let them know that I am here to help them and will get them to safety."

"Where will you take us?" she asked.

"I know some people that will help you."

Dax marched to the captain's seat and pulled out the two keys. He stuck the key into the ignition, and the yacht rattled as it started up. He then began to turn on switches as he placed the boat in reverse. The boat slowly started backing up. Dax looked and noticed the guards running toward the boat. He squinted his eyes and alerted all the girls.

"Get down!"

Several shots knocked against the hull.

Dax shot several arrows in the sky. The arrows soared through the air and quickly turned into nets, capturing the guards. Dax shot another arrow at the lighthouse guiding light that went through the bulb, turning the island dark.

"You all can get up now," Dax said.

The oldest girl slowly stood up and walked to the back of the boat. She found a refrigerator. Inside of the refrigerator was a twenty-four pack of bottled water. There was fresh fruit in a tray on a small table that she grabbed. She walked back up the stairs and began to hand out the fresh fruit to the girls. She went back down the stairs and retrieved the case of water. She placed the water down and walked over to a large chest that was unlocked. She removed the lock and opened the top. Her eyes stretched wide; she quickly grabbed something and closed the top. She looked at the stairs to see if anyone was coming.

Dax pulled out the phone that he'd taken from the captain. He looked to his side, and a bottle of water was being offered to him.

"Thank you."

"You're welcome. I gave them some fruit and snacks that I found in the small pantry. That should help them sober up. So where are you taking us?" she asked.

"Got it!" Dax exclaimed.

He began to press numbers on the phone and placed the phone on speaker.

"Hello?" a voice responded.

"Is this Trane?" Dax asked.

"Yeah, speaking."

"This is Dax. I need your help."

"What's up, Dax? I'm listening."

Dax looked at the young lady and took the phone off speaker. She slowly walked off and checked on the girls. She watched Dax as he steered the yacht and talked on the phone.

"Nina...are we going to be ok?" one of the girls asked.

"Yes...we're going to be fine," She replied.

Nina listened to Dax's muffled voice as he explained how he found the girls on the boat. Dax and Trane talked for several minutes before hanging up. Nina walked back to Dax and sat in the seat next to him.

"How are they doing?" Dax asked.

"They're in a safe space. I'm Nina."

"Nice to meet you, Nina. I'm Dax."

"So...where to?"

"Where meeting up with the BFA."

Chapter 19:

THE CORE

Dax and Nina got to know each other extremely well during their ride. Nina explained her decision that had led her to attending A and T. She explained that her grandmother had participated in a protest on February 3, 1960, a couple of days after the Greensboro Four sparked the courageous sit-in movement. She explained the unsung heroes, the Greensboro Four and the valor it took for them to organize and execute the counter sit-in. Dax was driven by her aspiration, and he knew that he had made the right choice by liberating the girls.

"So…the BFA. What is it?" Nina inquired.

"They are a group of brothers and sisters that are organized and willing to help their people from unjust acts. They will protect you and the girls. They will make sure that you receive the appropriate help. My cousin Staxx is one of the founding members; he told me, if I ever need help, to call them, not the police. We will meet with Trane; he's over at the west coast location."

Nina looked back at the girls and smiled. They all were sobering up from the drugs that they'd been injected with.

"We should be to the port in about fifteen minutes, and you should get the girls together and explain what's going on."

Nina gathered all the girls in a circle and started explaining who Dax was and how the BFA would reconnect them with their families.

A subtle classical tone came from the phone, followed by vibrating. Dax looked at the screen and answered the call.

"You will never get away with this. You think you can steal my yacht without repercussions? You will pay for this! You have twenty-four hours to return my boat."

"And then what?" Dax asked aggressively.

"If my yacht is not returned within twenty-four hours, along with my precious cargo, you're dead! Your whole family is dead!"

Dax ended the call and looked back at the girls; he smiled at them and nodded his head and subtly whispered to himself.

"God, guide my steps."

Dax approached a large port, and a bright light blinked on and off.

"That's him," he said to Nina.

The large boat pulled up to the side of the dock and stopped. Dax turned off the yacht and walked over to the girls.

"How's everyone doing?"

"A good night's rest in a warm comfortable bed would be great," Nina said. And then she chuckled.

"Trane is going to take really good care of everyone; he will provide you with everything you need tonight, and when the sun rises, he will start connecting you all back with your families."

Dax walked over to the three large anchors and lowered them into the water. He then walked to the side of the yacht and lowered the drawbridge. Trane was standing in the dark with three other men.

Dax walked off the yacht and greeted Trane.

"Long time, cuz," Dax said.

"Yeah, it has been a minute. What have you gotten yourself into?" Trane inquired, looking at the yacht.

"Good trouble," Dax said with a straight face.

"So...what do you have on board?"

Dax turned and looked up at the deck. Nina and all the girls were standing, listening to their conversation.

"These girls were abducted and were going to be used as sex slaves."

Trane looked at the girls.

"How many girls are there?"

"Fifteen."

"So, what do you want me to do with this?" Trane asked, looking at the yacht.

"I'm pretty sure you can find some use for it."

"Oh yea..." Trane said, rubbing his beard.

"Tech could change the computer system. I'm sure they have a tracker on it. I wouldn't want to bring my people more trouble. Ok, the girls can stay in our building; we have several beds available. Nurses are on duty as well. Let's get the girls inside and cover this baby up."

Trane was a leader; he knew exactly what to do and how to do it. The brothers started leading the girls off of the yacht one by one. Dax, Nina, and Trane were the last three on the yacht.

"There something I need to show you," Nina said to Dax.

She walked down the steps and showed Dax the large chest. After eying it for a moment, Dax opened it. Inside were war weapons. Military grade guns and ammo. Dax looked at Trane.

"Merry Christmas," Dax said as he lowered the lid.

They all walked off the yacht and headed into the building. Two brothers greeted them as they entered. A metal detector sounded off as they walked through the door. Nina slowly pulled out a handgun.

"I'm sorry. I forgot I had it on me," she said as she handed it to Trane.

"Nah, keep it," Trane said as he gently pushed her hand away.

Nina placed the gun back in her waist band and followed Dax and Trane.

Trane took them on a tour of the building and discussed the history of the BFA.

"So, are you guys like the Black Panthers?"

"We are definitely inspired by the Black Panther Movement. We take care of our own, and we police our own neighborhoods. We have our own schools, hospitals, grocery stores, libraries, etc. We are the community. We have several hubs; Tech handles the northeast hub, Malik controls the mid-west hub, and Quick handles the southeast hub," Trane explained.

They continued to walk through the building, admiring the independence of a black-owned community. Nina felt at home. Her black pride was welcomed at the BFA west-coast hub.

"What's this?" Nina inquired as she stopped to view a painting.

"What do you see?" Trane asked her.

"A picture of a black female, her hair is upheld in a natural style. She seems to be taking steps. Her complexion is a variety of colors, beauty. Her intuition is telling her to move forward. Her confidence is layered in her hair. The different shades of black are her ancestors that stand behind her and guide her doubted steps."

"That's deep. The girls will stay here," Trane said as he opened a door.

A tall, slender woman wearing glasses approached. She wore a white coat that stopped at her thighs. She greeted Nina with a welcoming smile and vibrant energy.

"Solei?" Dax asked as he tilted his head, confused.

Dax quickly opened his arms to embrace her with a welcoming hug.

"I haven't seen you in years! The last time I saw you, you were leaving home to attend college. What are you doing here?"

"Dr. Solei has been with us for about three years," Trane said.

"My bad! Dr. Solei," Dax said as they all laughed.

"Yes, after the COVID ran through the black community, I decided to leave the hospital and fight the virus on the ground. I followed my passion to educate my people on natural healing herbs, fruits, and vegetables to fight off the disease. I saw Trane at the ER one evening, and we just linked from there. He told me what he had going on with the hub and the great work they are doing for the community. It didn't hurt seeing a familiar face from home too. I went home that night and prayed for a sign to move forward. I received a sign that next morning and linked with Trane," Dr. Solei explained.

"It seems you two have some catching up to do. Nina…come with me. I'll show you where you can get cleaned up and get a hot meal," Trane said.

Trane and Nina left. Dr. Solei and Dax walked to her office.

"You have your own office, big time!" Dax said, and they both laughed.

Dr. Solei took off her coat and hung it on a coat rack.

"So, how's Cali treating you?"

"I love Cali. It's not home, but having my brother up here helps a lot. That is, when he's not hugging trees. I heard Granddad's voice in my head. I tried calling back home, but no one has returned my calls. What's going on, Dax?"

"Sol, there's a lot going on. There is too much to explain in one night. The girls that I brought here were sex slaves. I stole a boat from an island that they were transported to."

"What?"

"Yes, sex slaves. Staxx told me to reach out to Trane if I ever needed help, so I did. We are at war, Sol. You have to be extremely careful. There are a group of people, evil people called the soul seekers that are hunting us. They attacked Staxx and took his intern, Lauryn. Breeze, along with Myles, Seven, Blaze, Zaina, Night, Staxx, Fadez, and Que, went looking for Lauryn. I was with them, but I got sidetracked.

"Why is that?" Solei asked.

Dax just lowered his head; he was speechless.

"You are safe here. The brothers and I will protect you," Dr. Solei said as beams of solar energy flickered off of her arms, brightening the office. Dax placed his arm in front of his eyes to block the golden light. Solei's entire body began to glow, and Dax squinted to get a glimpse at her powers.

"That explains it! It was you all that time when we were younger."

"Yes, Granddad is the only one who knew about my powers. When I'm out in the sun, my powers are charged up. I have been doing research on the sun and its energy. It is amazing. The more knowledge I gain about solar energy, the more powerful I feel. I can literally touch an electric car with my finger, and it will fully charge. Every quarter, I take a trip to DC to the NASA headquarters to gain more access to my abilities."

They were suddenly interrupted by a knock at the door.

"Yes, come in," Solei said.

"The girls are all sleeping. We have nurses at every location to give them aid if needed. They were given some supplements to help with the withdrawal that they are experiencing," Trane said.

"Thank you, Trane. You really came through in the clutch."

"No problem. About the yacht...the brothers should be here in the morning to discuss what we will do with it. You should get some rest."

"I think I will. Let me check on Nina to see if she needs anything before I head out."

"Head out? Where are you going?"

"I'll sleep outside, on the hood of the yacht."

"Are you sure about that?" Trane asked.

"No...Let him be. He's been sleeping outside since we were kids," Solei said with a chuckle.

Dax left the room and went down the hall and saw Nina reading a book in her room.

"Hey, what are you reading?" Dax inquired.

"Tamika Mallory's book," Nina said showing Dax the cover.

"State of Emergency, sounds interesting. So, how are the girls?"

"They're all sleeping peacefully. Look, I don't know how I can ever repay you for your brave act of rescuing us."

"Stop. You don't owe me anything. As a black man, it is my duty to protect and provide for all of my sisters," Dax said to Nina as he reached for her hand.

Nina rubbed Dax's hands, admiring the roughness of his palms. Under each fingernail was a small layer of dirt.

"You are close with the earth. I like this tattoo."

"Thank you. This is my baby. A few of the guys and I left school early one day and went to Savannah, Georgia to get tattoos. I must have worn long sleeves for a week straight in the scorching month of July. I was so afraid of what my mother was going to say. It turned out I had totally forgotten about it and was walking around with my shirt off. She saw it and loved it!" Dax said, laughing.

Nina looked at the detailed art that covered Dax's entire left arm. The veins in his hands were outlined like the roots of a tree. The tree's body grew up his arm and branched out once it reached his shoulder.

"An oak tree. The king of the trees and the character of strength," Nina said.

"Yes," Dax said, surprised. He was astonished that Nina's perspective was aligned with his.

"Hey, I'm about to go and get some fresh air. I was just checking to see if you needed anything before I go?"

"Thank you for checking on me. I will be fine."

"Cool. Can I borrow one of your pillows? Sleeping on the hood of a boat without a head rest can be a recipe for a headache."

"Wait! You're sleeping on the boat and going stargazing? Count me in!" Nina said as she grabbed a blanket, a book, and the other pillow.

"All right…let's go," Dax said as Nina hurried out of the room, leaving him behind.

Nina walked down the hall to the exit. Two brothers with large guns let her pass as Dax followed.

"Hey, wait up!" Dax yelled.

Dax caught up with Nina and helped her onto the yacht. Nina laid out the blanket with the two pillows. Dax walked inside by the seat and retrieved his bow and arrows. Nina was already engaged with the night. She sighed as the stars shined above her.

"This is beautiful," Nina said.

"Look to your left. See that cluster of stars? They are the Maji Tribe. This bunch to your right is the Moto Tribe. The tribe beneath them is the Mnyama Tribe. The clusters far off in the corner are the Hewa Tribe. There you have the Jua Tribe. My ancestors are located toward the center, The Viumbe Wakuu Tribe."

"That's a different level of stargazing. Who taught you that perspective?"

"I spent several nights looking up at the stars and asking questions. The more you get in tune with nature the more the universe will answer your questions. Sometimes it just takes a quiet mind and peace. The universe will handle the rest," Dax said as he continued to gaze at the stars.

"The doctor—she seems like a very intelligent lady."

"Yes, Solei is extremely intelligent. She's my family; she will definitely make sure the girls are safe and get the proper help they need."

"What about you? How will you move going forward? Being abducted and all can bring a domino effect of trauma," Dax said.

Nina looked at the stars, trying to block out the thoughts that entered her mind. She closed her eyes tight. The images of the men who snatched her off the campus rushed through her mind. The captain's face plundered her peace. She began to inhale deeply and exhale. Dax looked at her and noticed she was struggling. He gently touched her hand and whispered to her.

"You are safe now."

Nina moved into Dax's arm as he consoled her. The negative thoughts that plagued her mind slowly passed through. Dax thought about the fellas and all the events that had taken place. He wondered if they were safe. In that moment, he felt a dose of guilt. Here he was star gazing with a potential soulmate, while his brothers were at war. This should have been a no-brainer, but Dax was conflicted, internally. He looked at Nina, who rested so peaceful in his arm. A subtle voice whispered, "Rest, my son. Restore your energy. When you awake, go to the House of Breeze."

"Thank you, God," Dax whispered.

"Who are you talking to?" Nina asked. She was awake, it turned out.

"I just received confirmation," Dax said as he gently pulled Nina close to him and closed his eyes.

He removed the device from behind his ear and took off his wristband, as he did not want to be disturbed.

Dax and Nina slept peacefully through the night until the first bird graced them with its presence. Dax opened his eyes and quickly grabbed his bow and arrow and drew back an arrow and pointed it. A man stood over Dax. Two TEC-9s were quickly drawn from the man's legs and pointed at Dax and Nina! Nina woke up and saw the gun pointed at her, and she quickly drew the handgun from her waist band and pointed it.

Solei heard the loud arguing outside and quickly ran to the noise. Trane, who was walking around the yacht, heard the arguing as well. Trane climbed up on the yacht and saw the two arguing.

"Yo, yo, yo! Put those things down before someone gets hurt."

"Trane, I think we have some squatters. What do you want me to do with them?"

"That's Dax! Man! Staxx and Quick's cousin."

"Who?"

"Dax from the hill."

Tech lowered his guns and placed them back in the holsters on his thighs. Dax put his bow and arrow down and stood up. Nina continued to point her gun at Tech, totally disregarding who he was. Tech had a black NY Yankee dad hat covering his eyes. He lifted the brim of his cap up, and Dax recognized him.

"Man, I almost filled you with holes," Tech said as he dapped Dax.

"Yeah, that wouldn't have ended well for you," Dax said as he laughed.

"My apologies. Is this your lady? I'm sorry for pointing a gun at you. I thought you were someone else."

Dax introduced the two: "Tech, Nina. Nina, Tech."

"Apology accepted," Nina said as she secured her gun.

"So, we have a stolen yacht that needs to be rewired," Tech said sarcastically.

He took off his backpack and pulled out a small tablet with wires.

"Where's the control room?"

"Right this way."

Dax and Tech walked to the control box, and Tech connected his tablet to the computer system and began doing his magic.

"How did you get the name Tech?" Dax inquired.

"Because I tote 2-TECs, and when I start to bust, I like to ask who's…" Tech sang in a deep voice. "Everyday struggle? Biggie? Never mind. Here, hold this for me."

Tech handed Dax the tablet and retrieved a small screwdriver from his backpack. He began unscrewing the panel underneath the steering wheel until it dropped onto the ground, making a clanking sound. He pulled out a small device with a flashing red light.

"Got it. This is a tracking device; I'm going to send it on a detour. They probably have already tracked it by now, though."

"So, is this like a GPS?"

"Exactly. I'm going to scan the yacht for more devices. This should take about thirty minutes, then we'll be done here," Tech said.

Tech walked off with a scanner, scanning the yacht from top to bottom. Solei arrived on the yacht and greeted everyone. Nina and Solei began to talk about the girls and how they could locate their families. Trane and Dax sat in the driver's and passenger's seats and began to talk about what was next for the BFA.

"So, where are you headed from here?" Trane asked.

"I'm going to check out a few things before I leave."

"Well, if you are around tomorrow, swing back by. I'm doing a little something for Quick's birthday."

"I didn't know Quick was here too."

"Yes, he came late last night."

"Hey, you did good. Look at me! I don't know your mission, but whatever it is that God has for you, you are doing an excellent job fulfilling it. Stay grounded and know that you always have help. I will make sure all the girls are back with their families myself. Continue your mission; don't worry about them," Trane said.

Dax was speechless. He sat on the firm leather seat, looking ahead. He looked at Trane and dapped him up.

"Aw! Look at you two being all mushy," Quick said as he entered the lower-level room on the yacht.

Dax stood up and laughed. He was excited to see Quick, as it had been years since they'd last spoken.

"Good to see you, Quick."

"Likewise," Quick said.

"She's clean," Tech said as he walked back to where the others were. "I scanned her from top to bottom. This is the only device I found. It will be better if we terminate it. I set the system so it can be remotely driven from my tablet. Also, the new GPS system is updating and enabled to track any unwanted guest. I would suggest allowing the software to update for about another hour before actually driving it. Other than that, we're good here."

"You did all of that in thirty minutes?" Dax asked.

"More like twenty-two minutes," Tech said.

They all laughed. Nina and Solei approached and gave the fellas an update on the girls. As Solei talked, the sun rays bounced and shined on her golden skin. The bright morning transferred its energy onto Solei. Her vibrant energy bounced and transferred to the others. Her energy was necessary. As she continued to talk, the frequency increased with positive vibes. Dax saw how Solei's energy was having a positive effect on everyone. He looked at Nina and made eye contact with her. They both smiled as their energy connected. A cool breeze flew through the air, making contact with their faces.

"Aw, this breeze feels so good," Nina said.

Dax had totally forgotten about his mission but was suddenly reminded.

"I have to go," he said, looking Nina in her eyes. "Sol, do you know where Breeze's home is located?"

"Yes, it's about an hour from here."

"We need to go now."

Everyone was stunned and confused from Dax's abrupt change in demeanor. Dax walked over to Nina, and he noticed her eyes were filled with tears as she anticipated saying goodbye.

"This is not goodbye, only a brief departure. I will return, God willing," Dax said to Nina.

Dax gave Nina a hug, and she stepped into the moment and fully embraced it. Her soft arms gently rested on his brawny shoulders. She locked her fingers together on the back of his neck, gently rubbing wool-like hair. His muscular arms secured her waist as he gently glided his hands from her lower back up to her rhomboids. He moved his fingers in a slow, circular motion, releasing her stress and tension. Nina buried her face in his chest, leaving the outer layer of his shirt damp. Dax slowly pulled away from Nina and kissed her brow. He wiped the tears from her face with the side of his thumb as she forced the muscles in her face to form a smile.

"This is not goodbye," Dax said again.

"I'll walk you to your car," Trane said, attempting to break the awkwardness.

Trane, Dax, and Solei walked from the yacht to the back of the building.

"Hey, Trane. Thanks again for everything."

"Don't worry about it, bro. Like I told you, I will make sure all the girls are reunited with their families."

Trane gave both of them love and walked back to the front of the building.

"So, why Breeze's house?" Solei asked.

"I don't know just yet, but we need to get there ASAP."

Solei touched the hood of her car, starting the engine and unlocking the doors.

"Come on, get in. I know a shortcut we can take to beat the traffic."

The two traveled down a wooded area and landed on a backroad.

"We're getting close. Should we pull up in the yard or park from a distance?"

"His home is to the right, ahead."

Solei pulled up to Breeze's home and suddenly felt a low frequency of energy!

"What's wrong, Sol?"

"Something is not right."

"Stay here while I go check out the place."

Solei gave Dax a look that said, "Really?" They got out of the car; Dax admired Breeze's home and was in awe. The futuristic architecture complemented Breeze's taste, as there was no other home built like it. There were no neighbors for several blocks, which enabled them to view the vast canvas of land leading to the ocean. His landscape was neatly trimmed to perfection. The glass pavilion allowed them to see through the ultramodern house from the outside. As they approached the front, they heard loud music playing from the front door of the house. Solei looked up to the second floor and noticed several men vandalizing the inside. She tapped Dax and pointed. Dax noticed the men and immediately ran to the front door. The front door was slightly open. He opened the door to allow his body to squeeze through. The surround sound blasted "Inner City Blues" by Marvin Gaye. Dax looked back at Solei to inform her, and she was gone! He stepped back outside, looked up, and saw a white, radiant energy glowing around her body as she levitated in the sky. Solei stretched her hand to the sky, and sun rays rained down to her body! She touched the thick bulletproof window. The glass slowly melted, and she placed both hands on the window, which hastened the process. Her existence was not to be denied as she floated inside the room through the melted window. All three of the men stopped in their tracks. They looked at each other, expecting someone else to make the first move. Sweat drenched their clothes, and the paint on the walls began to melt. The room felt like Dallol, Ethiopia, in June.

"Are you looking for something?" Solei asked as the white glow from her body faded and revealed her face.

Her feet touched the floor, hissing from the hot temperature.

"The Core! I've heard stories about you. What an honor it will be to take you back with us," one of the soul seekers said as his eyes ignited red.

Down on the first level of the home, Dax approached an elevator. The music throughout the house continued to blast, and Dax saw two men searching a bedroom from a distance. He stepped away from the elevator and retrieved his bow and two arrows swiftly. One of the guys looked up. It was too late! Two arrows pierced through each hand, nailing him to the wall. The other guy noticed and took off running, fumbling over a nightstand. Dax followed him.

Down in the black aquatic, a guy was suddenly disturbed by a loud thump. He walked over to a tablet and turned down the soulful tune that hummed from the basement throughout the home. Solei looked up as the music lowered, and one of the guys rushed her! Solei stomped the floor with force, and a hole emerged from her feet, burning through the wood. Her body went through the hole, and she grabbed the man's feet and yanked him down! She began to soar in the air as he held on for dear life; the other two men came to his aid and attempted to pull him up. Dax noticed the guy hanging from a hole in the ceiling and Solei levitating in the room. He was confronted with a dilemma as the guy he was chasing ran to the basement door. Solei floated over to the hole in the ceiling and pulled all the men down. One by one, their bodies fell from the ceiling, shattering a glass table. The intruder that ran from Dax opened the door to the basement and ran down the stairs. He noticed the high-tech basement, which was under the sea. He saw a large shark that swam back and forth by the large window. A man slowly approached, and the intruder quickly turned around and found himself standing in front of a man wearing a dark red beanie and a black long sleeve thermal shirt. The intruder's eyes turned red as he reached for a steel bar nearby. The man slowly walked in his direction, and the intruder swung the bar wildly. The man dodged every attempt. He caught the bar and pulled it out of the intruder's hand. Clank! The bar hit the floor; the intruder backed up against the glass wall. The large shark hit the glass and quickly swam away. The man in white threw his arms back, and his soul stepped out of his physical form and grabbed the intruder's neck, lifting his feet off the floor. The soul was visible in a ghost form. The man's physical body remained standing with hollow eye sockets. The soul reached into the intruder's belt and retrieved a knife.

"Mmmmm!" The intruder grabbed the soul's hand, trying the break his hold. The soul gently slid the knife across the intruder's arm, opening his flesh. The soul walked through the glass wall into the ocean and began to tread the water. He released his grip from the intruder's neck and treaded back through the glass window. The soul slipped back into its physical form and bred life back into the man. The hollow eye sockets cleared.

He watched as the blood flowed through the ocean. The intruder panicked as the large shark was alerted to the fresh blood and headed in his direction. The large shark swiftly mauled the intruder's arm.

The man turned off the lights and walked up the stairs. He arrived on the main level of the home and noticed bright lights beaming from someone's hands.

"Who's there?" he exclaimed.

Two black arrows came soaring at him. His soul jumped out and caught both of the arrows. The soul dropped the arrows and went back into the body. The light from the hand faded, and Solei walked out of the shadow. Dax pulled out another arrow; he pulled it back on the string.

"Wait!" Solei exclaimed as she got a clearer look at the person.

"It's my brother," she said.

"Soul? I thought you were out of the country."

Soul hugged Solei and asked her if she was ok.

"I came back once I heard Granddad's voice. Breeze always lets me crash with him when I'm out this way."

"Dax." Soul greeted Dax while looking down at the intruders.

"Soul." Dax greeted him back as if there were some unresolved issues.

"What do we have here?" Soul asked.

"Soul Seekers—they were tearing up the place," Dax said.

The four soul seekers sat on the floor, defeated.

"They wouldn't talk, so I figure we clip them right here," Dax said.

Solei's fist began to glow with white radiant energy as she attempted to interrogate the soul seekers.

"Whatever they came for, they were not successful. They trashed the second level of this home. What did you come here for?" Solei exclaimed as her radiant energy got closer to a soul seeker's face.

Dax placed his bow and arrow back into the holster.

"They are looking for the golden daggers," Dax said.

One of the soul seekers got up. Solei quickly blasted him with a high beam of energy, burning off his hand.

"What golden daggers?" Solei asked.

"The three daggers have been secretly placed on your pathetic planet for centuries. The powers that be have called for all three and will not rest until all three are in his possession," one of the soul seekers explained.

"We need to go; I know a place that's safe. There we can receive the guidance we need," Soul said.

They took the soul seekers to the basement and tied them up.

"So, what's up with this safe place?" Dax asked.

"Stand back," Soul ordered as he pointed his fist outward.

A ring on his middle finger began to glow. A bright purple hole opened.

"We will be safe here. Let's go!" Soul said.

Dax stepped in first. Solei followed behind him. Last, Soul stepped in, and the portal closed.

Chapter 20:

THE FALLEN ANGEL RISES.

A small device flashed on the hood of the yacht. Quick walked over to it. A bracelet was nearby, and it also flashed. Quick picked up the small device and the bracelet and placed the device to his ear. The frequency that came from the device was distorted. He looked at the wristband. "Supreme Beings" flashed across the middle. Quick placed his fingers over the wristband and pulled it down to his wrist. The flash immediately stopped on the device, and the voice became clear.

"Dax…Pick up…Dax!" the voice said.

"Yo! This is Quick. Who am I speaking to?"

The Beings were confused. They all wondered why Quick was speaking for Dax.

"Quick…This is Breeze. Where is Dax?"

"He left with Solei to go to your house."

"Why do you have his communication device?"

"I found it on the hood of his yacht. Look, man! Does someone want to tell me what is exactly going on around here?"

"We will explain later. Keep this device on. Good talking to you, Quick," Breeze said.

Quick turned around, and Trane and Tech were standing there.

"How long have you two been standing there?" Quick inquired.

"Long enough to know that something big is going down," Tech said.

"Dax is with Soul and Solei; he's not telling me his location," Staxx said.

The sun had risen on the island, and the Beings began to move. The island was cold with an uncanny vibe which suffused the air. The Beings decided that staying together would work better; from their experience, splitting up always resulting in loosing someone. They all crouched down and viewed the wooded land of the island. Breeze pulled out a small drone that fit perfectly in the palm of his hand. He then activated a hologram from his wristband, which presented a small screen. The drone took off. The Beings viewed the screen as the drone flew overhead, mapping out the entire island and sending signals back to Breeze's screen. The drone approached a large building, which resembled a massive prison.

"She's there," Staxx said.

"Calculate the distance from our location to this location," Seven said.

Breeze began to type on the screen; he then enlarged the view.

"That's fifteen miles," Breeze said.

Static appeared on the screen as the hologram flashed on and off. The camera view displayed the drone taking a nosedive toward the ground. The Beings looked at the screen as it displayed a metal *S*-shaped object sticking out of the drone. Sand covered the drone as half of it was engulfed in the beach. Black boots left large prints in the sand as someone approached the drone and picked it up. Two bright red eyes appeared on the screen.

"Welcome. I hope you took the scenic route. We have been patiently waiting for your arrival. The pleasure will be all mine, snatching your limbs one by one from your bodies. Sadly, no one will remember you after this war is won by me and my army."

The drone was then positioned to the back of the person, which allowed the drone to capture several soul seekers chanting, "Lord Soulek! Lord Soulek! Lord Soulek!"

Breeze turned off the screen. The chanting echoed through the island, and the Beings looked at each other, defeated.

"Going head on will not be smart. We need to bypass the north and find a way to get into the building without them seeing us. Besides, Lauryn is inside," Que said.

The soul seekers chanted as the Beings discussed their strategy to move in on them.

"One of them is the bearer of the dagger. Find the dagger and bring it to me. Don't fail me!" Soulek said to one of the soul seekers.

Several of the soul seekers charged toward the woods with weapons. Soulek walked back into the prison. Queen Dahlia was at the entrance, waiting for him.

"Our guests have arrived."

"Good. Prepare the chamber for our guests. I want them all alive to witness their last days…Don't mess this up," Queen Dahlia said to Soulek.

Soulek went to a double wooden door and pushed them open. The Beings heard the soul seekers moving closer to them while they were in the woods. Night stepped in front of the Beings and removed his sunglasses. He looked up at the bright sun, and the daylight became dim. The moon slowly stole the sun's shine and transitioned the day into night. He walked back to the group and joined the circle they had formed.

"Take us out of here, Myles," Staxx said.

The soul seekers stopped and stumbled over one another as the unexpected nightfall distracted them. Crickets started chirping, and the nocturnal animals began to lurk in the brush. Myles teleported the Beings out of the woods! The soul seekers appeared in the open area, where the Beings were.

"They were right here, in this open area," one of the soul seekers said as sharpened blade sang as someone removed it from its scabbard. The sun slowly appeared in the sky, where the moon held a temporary shelter in front of it. A dark purple fog floated around the wooded land. Standing back-to-back were Seven and his sister Zaina. Zaina opened her frock and grasped her sword. The queen of Ghana's spirit ignited the sword as it glowed a red hue. Seven looked at the sword; he clenched his fist, and they both shone with a powerful energy! The soul seekers were stunned as they began to back up in fear.

"Attack!" one of the soul seekers yelled.

Zaina began to engage in battle, swinging the sword at her adversaries. Seven displayed his supreme martial-arts techniques while overpowering the soul seekers with counter attacks from his glowing fists. Myles teleported, an axe in each hand. He began slicing the soul seekers as more of them arrived.

"There are hundreds of them!" Myles said.

"Where are the others?" Seven asked.

"They're outside of the prison," Myles responded.

Zaina, Myles, and Seven backed up until their backs touched. They placed their weapons back into their holsters and discretely touched each other.

"Let's go, Myles," Seven said.

"I can't!" Myles said.

"What do you mean?" Zaina asked.

"I don't know. It feels like there's a force that's holding me back."

The soul seekers all retreated as the ground began to shake. The Beings looked at the ground; the fallen leaves from the trees trembled as a hole sucked at the earth. Seven levitated off the ground and used his powers to bring Zaina and Myles with him moments before the earth was snatched from under their feet. A few of the soul seekers fell into the hole and hung onto tree roots for dear life. A large veiny hand appeared out of the hole; its fingernails were painted grey. The hand had dirty linen wrapped around its knuckles that expanded to the forearm. The person pushed himself out of the abyss, revealing his head. His straight black hair covered his ears; the death in his eyes was as dark as the hole he crawled out of. He lifted himself onto the land, displaying his strength, as four soul seekers held to his waist and legs. The soul seekers immediately bowed down upon his arrival. He stood up, and the earth's hole closed.

"Salvo...The Fallen Angel," Seven whispered.

He brushed the ashes off of his bronze flesh. He stood six feet, seven, with a mesomorph body shape. The Fallen Angel looked at the Beings levitating. He swiftly spread his wings and knocked Myles and Zaina from the air. His wings' feathers were black like a raven's. He knelt down and stuck his hand in the dirt. He pulled a large sword from the earth and began to strike at Myles and Zaina. Myles quickly pulled Zaina and teleported away from the deadly strikes. The Fallen Angel moved towards Myles as though anticipating his every move. When Myles appeared, the Fallen Angel grabbed his neck! Zaina delivered a blow to the back of the Fallen Angel, clipping his right wing. The Fallen Angel released Myles and swung his angelic blade at Zaina!

The blade whistled through the air and landed on Seven's glowing forearms! Seven stepped in front of Zaina, blocking the blade with his forearms, creating an "X." Seven's entire arm beamed a golden power. The Fallen Angel summoned strength from the Dark Realm, which enabled his angelic blade to catch fire! His tar-colored eyes turned into fire as he pressed down on Seven's arms, displaying his evil force. A dark purple fog appeared out of the atmosphere. Myles came soaring down, with his right arm cocked back, his fist radiating a dark-blue energy!

His fist connected with the Fallen Angel's face, shifting his facial structure. The Angel dropped his sword, giving Seven the split second to use his golden fists. The Angel flew back but quickly regained his advantage by flapping his left wing. He looked down at his chest, which displayed two fist prints from Seven's energetic blast. He then looked back at his right wing, which was slowly regenerating. A soul seeker tried picking up the angelic blade, and his skin began to melt! His flesh oozed over his bone while he screamed in agony. The Fallen Angel leaped over to the soul seeker and pulled his hand off of the blade.

"You are not worthy to summon the dark force," The Fallen Angel said as he grasped his blade.

Myles, Seven, and Zaina wasted no time. They quickly teleported away from the Fallen Angel and the soul seekers. Zaina opened her eyes, and they were at the back of the large prison. Staxx, along with the other Beings, looked on as Zaina, Myles, and Seven breathed deeply.

"What happened?" Fadez asked.

They all heard a loud flapping sound, like the wind connecting to the main sail of a sailboat. They looked up and observed the large black wings landing on top of the prison.

"What was that?" Fadez asked.

"That's Salvo the Fallen Angel, leader of the Dark Realm. He appears on earth once every blue moon. Legend has it that he was one of God's angels that protected the pearly gates. His thirst for power and dominance drove him to try and overpower God. God cast him from the sky above. From there, he roamed and ruled the Dark Realm. Legend has it, he has made some of the most ferocious weapons. He's a master armorer and master swordsmith. He is able to endure extremely hot temperatures and summon an army of evil," Seven said.

"How do you know so much about this…Salvo, Fallen Angel?" Blaze inquired.

"I have traveled the world; I gain most of my knowledge about him from a reliable source in Cairo."

Fadez reached into his waistband and pulled out Blaze's bow.

"You might want to hold onto this," Fadez said.

"Let's go and get Lauryn," Que said.

The Fallen Angel entered through a door at the top of the building. There, he was greeted by soul seekers.

"How can we assist you, my Lord?"

"Take me to Queen Dahlia."

The soul seekers walked down the long dark hall. The Fallen Angel walked behind them, keeping about five feet away. They arrived at Queen Dahlia's layer and knocked on the large door. The large door slowly opened, and the soul seekers stepped to the side as the Fallen Angel walked through the door. The Queen sat in a large chair; on her right stood Mungo, and on her left stood Soulek. The Fallen Angel approached the throne. He gently spiked his angelic blade on the stone floor, creating little sparks from the razor point. He grasped the pommel and kneeled down on one knee. Soulek looked down at the angel's wings, observing that one wing was larger than the other.

"Rough landing?" Soulek sarcastically asked.

"Lord Salvo, The Fallen Angel, ruler of the Dark Realm, rise," Queen Dahlia said.

He slowly rose with his eyes on Soulek; he then moved his hand from the pommel to the grip of the sword. Mungo followed his hands, admiring the angelic blade.

"Rough landing? No. Inconvenience due to your failure? Yes," Lord Salvo replied.

"A leather carbon-fiber grip that is custom-fit for the palm. The cross guard replicates your wings when they are extended. A black blade—I have never laid eyes on such a masterpiece," Mungo said.

"Your details are precise; many wars have been won with the doubled-edged angelic blade. I've seen you have found the second Golden Dagger. Please accept this gift as a token of your labor," Lord Salvo said.

He reached behind his wings and pulled out a sleet carbon-fiber glove. He handed the glove to Mungo and instructed him to put it on his right hand. Mungo accepted the glove and did as he was instructed.

"How does it feel?"

"It feels normal, like any other glove," Mungo responded.

"Good. Now touch your index knuckle."

Mungo touched his knuckle, and steel spikes sprang from the entire outer layer of the glove.

"You see? Each knuckle unleashes a close combat weapon," Lord Salvo explained.

Mungo pressed his middle knuckle, and four lightning claws slid out of each knuckle. Mungo created a fist and examined each claw.

"Gently touch the center of the glove."

Mungo touched the center of the glove, and the claws slid back into the knuckles.

"We will need you to win this war," Lord Salvo said to Mungo.

Mungo moved his fingers and continued to examine the glove. He liked the glove, but his greed craved the angelic blade. Dahlia reached down and pulled out a long box from the side of the throne.

"Since we are all in the giving mood, this gift is for you..."

Lord Salvo placed his angelic blade on the cold stone floor and received the box from his Queen. He opened it and pulled out a scabbard.

"Now your angelic blade can rest properly, when it is not beheading or slicing throats."

Mungo's eyes widened as Lord Salvo placed the blade in the scabbard. Lord Salvo wrapped the leather strap around his head, left arm, and left wing. Dahlia stood up and assisted him with making it snug on his chest. She gently rubbed his bare chest and smiled. This was tradition for the soul seekers to exchange gifts before battle. Soulek was devastated. He thought about his missions and journeys that were fulfilled. Rage and deceit filled his soul. Lord Salvo stepped to the side while Dahlia went back to the throne; she then pulled out another box.

"Soulek, my loyal and most honorable soldier. You have proven yourself worthy to endure the name Lord. From this day forth, you shall be referred to as Lord Soulek!"

Lord Soulek opened the box and pulled out a sword.

"Thud!" They looked back and noticed a spear head poking through the wooden door. Lightning flashed from the spear head, and the door exploded!

Chapter 21:

THE DAGGER BEARER

Blaze walked through the entrance and picked up his spear, which lay with the debris from the wooden door. The other Beings walked in behind him, each of them holding their weapons. The room was large with stone flooring and cold brick walls, which the air bounced off of. Lord Salvo stood in the middle, with Mungo on his right and Lord Soulek on his left. Mungo clenched his battle fist, and the lightning claws ejected out. Lord Soulek grasped his soul blade, and Lord Salvo remove the angelic blade from the scabbard.

"Where's Lauryn?" Blaze asked.

"Lightning Boy!" Mungo said.

"Where is Lauryn?" Blaze repeated. This time, he charged his spear with lightning.

"You cannot get in the way of what destiny has in store," Lord Soulek snarled.

Zaina noticed the large throne the three protected. Queen Dahlia sat comfortably on the throne, sheltered by her allegiance.

"Why don't you show yourself!" Zaina yelled out.

"You must be Doc's heirs," The Queen said as she stood up.

Lord Salvo stretched his wings to protect her.

"I'm fine, my Lord," she said as she stepped in front of Lord Salvo, revealing herself to the Beings.

"It's her. She hasn't aged a bit," Fadez whispered, remembering the picture from Doc's journal.

"Welcome to my domain. I take it, you all have come to save the souvenir. Who's the dagger bearer?" Queen Dahlia asked as she examined them all.

Fadez immediately looked at the floor, trying to appear normal. Queen Dahlia looked at Fadez and gazed into his eyes. Her beauty compelled him to put down his guard. She looked at his right ankle and noticed something bulging out to the side.

"The young and handsome! Hand over the Golden Dagger, and you will experience a quick death. I call it mercy," The Queen said.

The Beings looked at Fadez, confused. Staxx looked on the side of the throne and noticed someone on the ground wearing a hospital gown. He noticed the legs slowly moving.

"Ivy..." Staxx whispered under his breath.

"Bring the handsome boy to me!" The Queen said as she went back to her seat.

"Soul seekers!" Lord Soulek yelled out.

Several soul seekers came from the rear and the side entrance of the large room. Mungo locked in on Blaze and walked down the steps. Lord Salvo tried to grab Mungo to hold him back.

"Let him go...He has the heart of a pawn," Dahlia whispered to Lord Salvo.

Lord Soulek stared at Dahlia from his peripheral, eavesdropping. The soul seekers charged the Beings and engaged in battle. Blaze led the Beings into battle, striking first. He disengaged the tip of his spear and struck the floor, sending an electrical shock wave at the soul seekers. Mungo stumbled but quickly recovered his posture and engaged in battle with Blaze. Mungo swung a vicious hook with his battle fist. Blaze blocked it with his bow and countered with a one-two paralyzing, shocking jab. Seven stood back and locked on Lord Salvo. He didn't blink his eyes or move when the soul seekers came his way. Instead, he countered all their attacks and sent energy blasts from his fists, while focusing on Lord Salvo.

"Impressive," Lord Salvo said, trying to spot a weakness in Seven's ability.

Night flipped around the room and engaged in close combat with his crescent moon knives. He spun the moon knives around as he slashed the arms of the soul seekers. Night moved swiftly, swinging the moon knives and slitting ankles of the soul seekers. Once they dropped to the floor, he delivered fatal slashes to their throats. Que clutched the grip of his simi sword, and it ignited into a bright orange flame. Two soul seekers with swords approached Que and Staxx. Que, with his sword on fire, sparred with the soul seeker as Staxx joined. Staxx pulled the small dagger from his Achilles' heel and threw it at the soul seeker. The dagger landed in his chest, which slowed him up. Que followed with a scorching swing of his blade that penetrated the flesh of the soul seeker and separated his bones. Myles pulled out his two axes.

"Time to see what you can do," Myles said.

He threw the two axes that targeted the heads of two soul seekers, who were charging him from the front. He then teleported to the left side of the room. The soul seekers turned their heads halfway in search of Myles. The axes sliced through the two heads and boomeranged back to Myles's hand. Myles looked at the gloves and the axes.

"That's enough," Lord Soulek said as he walked down from the throne.

He pushed his foot soldiers out of the way to get to the nearest Being within arm's reach. Lord Soulek snatched Que from behind and tossed him against the wall! Que's face collided with the brick wall, which instantly knocked him unconscious. Lord Soulek lifted his soul blade to deliver a death blow to Que! Night threw one of his moon knives at the soul blade and knocked it out of Lord Soulek's hand! The heavy metal sword and crescent moon knife dropped to the stone floor, igniting sparks. Lord Soulek reached down to pick up his sword, and Fadez ran over to him and delivered a kick to the side of his face! The impact from the kick sounded throughout the room. The Queen looked on at Fadez as she admired everything about him.

"Bring him to me," She said to Lord Salvo.

Lord Salvo was waiting for his turn to be unleashed. He noticed Seven still watching his every move. Lord Salvo pulled out the angelic blade, spread his large wings, and glided down from the throne. Seven engaged the hands of God and slowly began to walk toward Lord Salvo.

"We meet again," Lord Salvo said to Seven.

He swung the blade at Seven's head, in an attempt to deliver a death strike. Seven quickly completed a back flip to dodge the death strike. He saw the type of energy Salvo was transferring, so he matched it with a quick one-two jab with the power from above. Staxx communicated with Myles by using his telepathy powers.

"I think Lauryn is behind the throne. Can you get there?" Staxx's thoughts transferred to Myles.

Myles glance at Dahlia, who sat on the throne; he then noticed more soul seekers running out from the back.

"Just cover me," Myles said.

Mungo and Blaze continued their feud as they fought blow for blow. Zaina saw that Mungo was getting the best of Blaze. Mungo engaged his spike fist and started delivering body blows to Blaze's ribs. Zaina walked over to Mungo and noticed he had the sword she'd given Ivy.

"I believe that blade belongs to me," Zaina said, removing her hood.

Mungo gazed at her and was suddenly distracted by her sword. Zaina gripped the sword and embraced the powers of Yaa Ashantewaa! Blaze breathed heavily as he dodged a right uppercut from Mungo. Blaze used his bow to strike Mungo on the side of his neck. A bone in Mungo's neck dislocated! Mungo fell to the ground, holding the side of his neck in pain. With his head leaning to the side, he placed his left hand on top of his head and his right hand beneath his chin. He pushed his left hand to the right and his right hand in the southwest direction! The dislocated bone snapped back in place. Mungo stood up and pulled the blade he'd taken from Ivy out of his waistband. Zaina charged Mungo and began to scrap with him. Blaze joined in by taking out Mungo's legs with his bow. Mungo dropped the blade, and Zaina quickly kicked it out of his reach. Zaina did just enough to get Dahlia's attention. Myles teleported behind the throne, where he found Ivy untying Lauryn. Ivy looked at Myles, surprised at his sudden arrival.

"Here, let me help," Myles said as he cut the restraints with his small axe.

"Look out!" Ivy yelled as several soul seekers charged them.

Myles quickly turned around to fight off the soul seekers, but there were too many of them. Staxx arrived to assist Myles. He glanced at Ivy and Lauryn. Ivy took the cloth and gag out of Lauryn's mouth.

"Staxx!" Lauryn yelled.

Dahlia stood up from the throne once she heard Lauryn's voice. She took off her top-layer gown and one step forward. She was startled by a black metal star that landed on the head of the throne. She noticed Zaina approaching her. Dahlia gracefully walked down from the throne and pulled out a blade. The sharp edge sparkled with a rose-gold hue. The cross guard was gold etched with flowers. Zaina had never seen a weapon with so much grace and elegance. Zaina looked at Dahlia, who was clothed in a body suit that hugged her figure, displaying all of her unique curves. The hieroglyphics on her heels conveyed that she was a queen warrior. Dahlia charged toward Zaina with the rose-gold blade. Their swords whined through the air before clashing. Sparks from the blades colliding brightened the dusky room.

"The Blade of Deceit has been my weapon of choice for many centuries. Many kings and queens have been lured in by my goddess aura. Yet they fall short of the Blade of Deceit," Dahlia said as she clashed her blade with Zaina's blade.

"Being able to foresee my every move is a skill that you lack," Dahlia said.

Dahlia maneuvered around Zaina until she landed a kick to her stomach. Zaina dropped her sword and dodged a lunge from the Blade of Deceit. Zaina countered with a left hook while spinning around Dahlia. Dahlia quickly turned around to face her opponent. Zaina pulled a Golden Dagger from Dahlia's holster, and she gracefully slid the dagger up from Dahlia thigh to her midsection. Dahlia shouted in anguish.

Her unblemished, brown skin opened to display her off-white flesh as her blood immediately covered her wound. Lord Salvo soared and kicked Seven in the chest with his feet. He glided to his Queen and lifted her up off the ground. Zaina ran, jumped, and pulled them back to the ground. The three begin to tussle as Fadez arrived to help Zaina. Dahlia retrieved the Golden Dagger from Zaina as Lord Salvo thrust her away with his wing!

Ivy tried her best to remove the gloves from Lauryn's hands, but they were secured tight. After Staxx and Myles fought off the soul seekers from the rear, they went back to Ivy and Lauryn. Staxx ran and hugged Lauryn.

"I'm sorry I failed to protect you. Let's get you out of here," Staxx said.

Myles and Staxx looked at the gauntlets that covered Lauryn's hands. They tried pulling them off and cutting the restraints with the axes. The metal was too durable.

Fadez grabbed Dahlia while she was on the ground. Breeze blasted Lord Salvo out of the sky with powerful ultramarine energy flares! Fadez looked in Dahlia's eyes as he let down his guard; she too was drawn to Fadez as she relaxed her muscles. Dahlia slowly caressed Fadez's leg; he closed his eyes at the sensation that he felt from her soft warm hand. Breeze saw Fadez with his eyes closed.

"Faaaadez!" Breeze yelled.

Dahlia snatched the other dagger from her holster, and with the dagger she'd regained from Zaina, she stabbed Fadez's rib cages. She tossed Fadez off of her, and his back connected with the cold floor. Dahlia rolled over and snatched the holster from Fadez's ankle with the dagger inside.

"Fool, you made this too easy," Dahlia said as she snatched the two daggers out of Fadez's side.

"Lord Salvo. Open the portal to the Dark Realm!" Dahlia yelled out.

Lord Salvo, Mungo, and Lord Soulek made their way to their Queen. Lord Salvo's wings spread wide and created a shield that covered them. The Beings ran to Fadez. A large black sphere opened behind the large wings, and they escaped inside. The portal closed. Silence entered the room as the Beings stood around Fadez. His wounds were not healing at the rapid pace he was used to.

"The Golden Daggers that she stabbed him with are having an effect on his healing ability," Zaina said as her hands glowed and hovered over the wounds.

Staxx, Myles, Ivy, and Lauryn walked out from behind the throne. Que and Night walked over to Lauryn, their bodies battered and beaten. Que and Night hugged Lauryn tight and noticed the heavy gauntlets that covered her hands. Seven walked over to Lauryn and noticed the engravings on the gauntlets.

"These symbols represent fire and ice. Are you able to move your fingers?" Seven asked Lauryn.

"No, I'm not," Lauryn answered.

Seven held the gauntlets, and his hands began to glow as his power increased; the restraints cracked off. Lauryn immediately pulled her hands out of the gauntlets, and they fell to the ground, cracking the stone floor. The Beings looked at Lauryn's hands. Her left hand blazed a scorching flame, and her right hand was suddenly covered in a thick layer of ice. The artic mist from her hand soared through the room. Fadez sat up with the aid of Zaina, and they both looked at the fire and ice emerging from Lauryn's hands.

"Light! I need light."

Lord Salvo grabbed a torch stick and lit it. The fire from the tip of the stick gave light to the Dark Realm. Mungo, Lord Soulek, and an injured Queen Dahlia stood in a cave-like realm. Dahlia fell to her knees and pulled the three daggers out of her holsters. Lord Salvo moved the torch to illuminate the daggers.

"Noooooooooo!" Dahlia screamed as she looked at the two golden daggers and the steel dagger that she'd snatched from Fadez's ankle.

Doc picked up his wooden staff and moved it in a circular motion. A large portal opened with a bright white light. Brix and Egypt held their arms up to the bright light as Doc walked into the portal. Doc held out his hand, gesturing for Brix and Egypt to enter. Brix held Egypt's hand as they walked into the portal together. Doc was greeted by five elders; they all were dressed in long robes. An elder lady held her hand out. Doc reached for her hand, and tears fell from his eyes.

"My sister," Doc said as they all walked.

Doc, Brix, and Egypt were led to a beautiful room. Doc, his sister, and the other elders left the room and walked to an open area. Three large men with wings and swords guarded a door. They greeted Doc, his sister, and the elders with a nod. They stepped to the side and opened a door, and a bright light escaped from the room as Doc and his sister walked in. The sister walked to a large mantle with a large chest. She unlocked the chest and lifted the top.

Doc's eyes widened as he saw the golden dagger.

They heard someone walking toward them, and they turned around and it was Dax.

"Thank you, son," Doc said to Dax.

Doc closed the large box, and the elders, along with Soul, Solei, Brix, and Egypt, walked in.

"We have to get the other two daggers," Doc said.

"We don't have enough power to get them," Brix replied.

A beautiful angel walked over to them; their souls were instantly warmed from her smile. She walked over to Brix and touched his shoulder.

"Be encouraged," she said softly.

Lauryn began to feel a power that she had never felt, and she pushed her arms out. The fire and ice mixed together and birthed a large portal. The Beings looked at the portal, and they could hear Queen Dahlia screaming from beyond.

ABOUT THE AUTHOR

Damon Thompson was born and raised in Beaufort, South Carolina. He earned a BS in Human Services at The University of South Carolina at Beaufort, and an MS in Human Services at Capella University. After starting his professional career at Robert Smalls Middle School where he served as a behavioral intervention specialist, he now works with youth and their families to provide multi-systemic therapy. From a young age, Damon loved to create characters and bring them to life. After the birth of his second daughter, he decided to put his creative thoughts into action and begin writing his first novel, *Supreme Beingz: Finding The Inner G*, which was published in 2019. In his spare time Damon enjoys listening to music from jazz to hip-hop. He also has a passion for the outdoors and nature as it inspires him to write. He currently resides in North Carolina, with his wife and two daughters.

CPSIA information can be obtained
at www.ICGtesting.com
Printed in the USA
JSHW050041110323
38805JS00005B/18